# The Sheikh's

# Reluctant American

## By Leslie North

### The Adjalane Sheikhs Series

### Book 3

# Blurb

Banished Sheikh Malid Adjalane has no interest in returning to the family business under the watchful eye of his controlling father. But if Malid doesn't agree to take on a tough deal, he won't be allowed into the palace to see his dying mother. With no other choice, Malid finds himself deep in negotiations with the largest oil producer in the world. He expected hard work, but he never could have prepared himself for the gorgeous, ambitious woman on the other end of this business deal.

Nigella Michaels works hard for her father's oil company, but she still has a lot to prove. It's a masculine industry, and with her dad about to retire, this deal could be just what she needs to show him once and for all that she's the right person to continue his legacy. She's always worked well with others, and this should be no exception. But not even her meticulous research could have prepared Nigella for the instant attraction she has with Malid.

After so many years on his own, it won't be easy for Malid to put up with his father's terms. But with Nigella's help, perhaps they'll both learn to balance the weight of their family with their own desires.

# Dedications

I dedicate this book to you, my loyal readers. Thank you for all the lovely e-mails, reviews, and support. Without you, this wouldn't be possible.

Thank you for downloading 'The Sheikh's Reluctant American (The Adjalane Sheikhs Series Book Three)'

Get <u>FIVE</u> full-length, highly-rated Leslie North Novellas <u>FREE</u>! Over 548 pages of best-selling romance with a combined <u>421</u> FIVE STAR REVIEWS!

Sign-up to her mailing list and start reading them within minutes:

# Table of Contents

# Chapter 1

Malid Adjalane could feel Fadin's stare on him, but he kept his eyes on the sand that stretched before them. Trust the security guy to worry. It was best to get over such shifting ground fast, and Fadin knew that. But he didn't look comfortable. He gripped the door rest of the SUV with white knuckles, and Malid had to smile. Fadin had taught him to drive, but the older man was a cautious soul. Malid wasn't. Not right now at least.

Fadin broke the silence between them. "We crossed back into Al-Sarid two miles back."

Giving a nod and a shrug, Malid lifted a hand from the wheel. Fadin knew why they were making this drive. Fadin had been with Malid for years, even through the exile that Malid's father had imposed. Right now nothing was going to keep Malid from getting to his mother's side—even if that meant he had to jump to his father's orders.

However, as expected, Fadin's dark eyes sharpened. Irritation pulled his mouth down. He looked younger than his sixty years. Gray had only started to show at the temples of his dark hair, which he wore close-trimmed. His beard was also close shaven—Fadin didn't like anything that might be used against him in a fight.

Fadin gave a disapproving sniff—or Malid was going to guess it was disapproving. Fadin hadn't liked the idea of this return to Al-Sarid. "I hope you have no intention of trying to meet all your father's demands. Whatever they are, you can be sure he has something else hidden."

Malid shrugged again. He had no illusions about his illustrious father, Sheikh Nimr, head of the Adjalane family, and one of the most powerful men in Al-Sarid. Nimr was a tyrant both in the boardroom of the family company and within the family. He and Malid had never seen eye to eye, and Malid was not about to be sucked back into his father's world of control. But he would also not allow his father to stand in the way of what was owed to family.

Next to him, Fadin studied the landscape. The deserts of Al-Sarid could be beautiful—distant mountains of purple, shifting white dunes dotted with small clumps of grasses and palms near the springs that made travel possible across the hot lands. Al-Sarid hugged the coast of Arabia—a tiny sliver of a country that relied more on tourism dollars than on oil, but the land did have a huge asset. Access to the coast.

Voice gruff, Fadin said, "Opell Oil will want their pipeline to be low cost construction—that means Adjalane land, which has the best water, the best level ground."

Hands tight on the steering wheel, Malid pushed out a breath. He hadn't told Fadin everything about the phone call he'd had with his father—things within the Adjalane family were…complex. They had been between Malid and his two brothers, and between Malid and his father. Too much pride, perhaps, Malid thought. His mouth twisted. He wasn't above having that same problem.

Glancing at Fadin, Malid gave in—Fadin would keep poking and making comments until Malid answered his questions. That kind of dogged pursuit was a good trait in a head of security, but it was also sometimes irritating.

"Yes, Opell Oil wants a pipeline, and my father asked me to handle the matter."

Fadin nodded. "Asked because he wants you to prove something?"

Malid shook his head, but this was something of a peace offering—or at least that was how it appeared on the surface. Malid had butted heads with his younger brother, Adilan, over regaining a piece of land—an oasis called Al-Hilah. Adilan had gotten the land back into the family by marrying the American woman whose mother held the deed. A nice trick that. Mouth sour, Malid clenched his back teeth. Nimr had not approved of some of Malid's plans to acquire the land by other means, and had thought the charges Malid had brought against that American were…dishonorable. As if such a matter of business was any place for honor.

However, now Nimr needed Malid's business skills— Adilan was too busy with his new wife and other matters, Nassir was terrible at negotiations, and Malid had not enjoyed his time away from his homeland. This seemed a good opportunity for everyone.

Topping a sand dune, Malid slowed the vehicle. Below, on rocky ground at the edge of the dunes, two off-road

vehicles with thick tires—much like on Malid's SUV—
were parked on a narrow track. Malid could see three
people—two with survey equipment.

"Opell Oil?" Fadin asked. He didn't sound pleased.
"They seem to think they own this land already."

Putting the SUV in gear, Malid drove down the dune
and parked near other vehicles. At least these people knew
enough to bring in desert equipment. Glancing at Fadin,
Malid told him, "See what you can learn from the
surveyors—I'm looking for any leverage in this deal. I
must meet with the woman in charge."

"Woman?" Fadin paused, one hand on the door.
"Gordon Michaels sent a woman to negotiate?"

"Not just a woman. Gordon Michaels may own Opell
Oil, but the woman in question is Nigella Michaels…his
daughter. I expect we are both being tested by our
parents."

Fadin muttered a curse, and Malid had to agree with it.
Family businesses ought to be more business and less
family—or that was how Malid felt at times.

Getting out of the air conditioned SUV, Malid shaded his eyes. The sun and heat hit him at once—a welcome to his home. He had grown up in these deserts—he loved the heat. But he also knew the dangers. He grabbed a cap to better shield his eyes and adjusted his sunglasses.

Nigella Michaels stood out at once. She held a map in her hands and stood with her back to him. She had to have heard the SUV's engine, but she wasn't paying any attention to it—that showed a certain confidence, or perhaps a certain recklessness. Bandits weren't unknown in the desert.

Jeans encased long legs, and his first thought was she was like a gazelle—lean and graceful. Her head was uncovered—not wise in the desert, but it gave him a view of deep brown, almost black, waves. She turned and pulled down her sunglasses, giving him a glimpse of eyes the color of amethysts. Her complexion was perfect, and the white shirt she wore offered up a hint of the cleavage that lay underneath.

Nigella was a beautiful woman, and a surge of interest swept through him. He frowned. An attraction was not a complication he wanted—not when it came to business.

*I've been without a woman for too long.*

Well, nothing to be done about that just now. He strode to her side and held out his hand. "Nigella Michaels?"

She kept staring at him over the top of her sunglasses and she was frowning. "You must be an Adjalane. I don't know who else would have that hawk nose or be able to track me down out here. So which one are you? The one who just got married, the one into sports, or the banished son?"

\*\*\*

He smiled—it changed his face. She'd seen photos of Sheikh Nimr Adjalane—part of her homework to make this deal happen—and this guy looked a lot like him. Serious expression—or that's what he'd just had—and black hair peeking out from under a ball cap that shaded his face. His hair was slightly too long in the back, giving him a rakish appearance that reminded her of the stories of marauding sheikhs who captured young women and carried them off to their desert lairs. He was clean shaven, but it looked as if his beard was about to grow back—it shadowed his jaw and cheeks. He was dressed in khakis and boots—so was the other guy with him—but they were crisp, clean and left Nigella feeling sweating and rumpled.

"Not so banished now. I'm Malid. And this is Adjalane property. Aren't you getting ahead of yourself?"

Nigella smiled. "Ah, Malid Adjalane. You're the one they booted for lying. I'd heard your father never intended to see your face again." She wanted to see if she could shake him—it was always good to find out just who you were dealing with.

His own smile didn't fade, but it did stiffen. "Actually, I am here at my father's request." He waved a hand at her surveyors. "The question is what are you doing out here when access has not yet been arranged?"

Tucking her map into her messenger back, Nigella said, "It's best to have some kind of idea just what we're negotiating for."

"You plan to put the pipeline through here?" Malid asked.

"That depends on your family, doesn't it?"

Malid took a step closer. Nigella's heart kicked up a little—the guy was good looking and obviously knew it. She didn't trust him an inch. "You're very blunt," he said. "I like that."

She thought about telling him she didn't give a rat's ass what he liked, but she was supposed to play nice here. Holding her ground, she looked him up and down, from the starched collar of his shirt to the laces of his boots— nice ones, leather and American made if she knew her boots. "Banishment seems to agree with you."

"My father asked me to absent myself from Al-Sarid— he didn't condemn me to a life of poverty. My palace is just over the border."

The words came out so easily, and Nigella wondered if he realized how crazy his last statement was. *My palace.* He really was just like something out of some kind of desert fantasy—the gorgeous, brooding sheikh with a past and his wounds. She wished she could see his eyes to know if he was having her on, or was he really serious about all of this.

Sweat trickled down her face—and her back. She didn't wipe it away. She wasn't from this part of the world—not that it couldn't get hot in Texas—and she was determined to earn the respect of not just her dad, but everyone in the business. This was her chance to prove she could cut tough deals in the Middle East.

Malid lifted a hand and wiped a drop of sweat from her cheek. "You have not adjusted to our climate yet."

She pushed her sunglasses back in place and turned away slightly. Her pulse was jumping and she was hoping the heat on her skin really was just the desert. "I don't think any amount of time here would get me used to these temperatures. And it's only ten."

"You would be wise to stay indoors during the hottest part of the day—that is what we do. With your fair complexion, you would burn easily. And that, Ms. Michaels, is why you should cover your head—a scarf, a hat, or anything is better than no protection from the sun."

Nigella's cheeks warmed even more. She'd been trying to make a statement with her Western clothing—she wasn't going to look second class here. But it seemed she'd just shown herself not to be all that smart. She gave a nod. "I'll think about that. And, please…it's Nigella."

Stepping back, Malid gestured to his SUV. It was black, big, and looked more like a military vehicle. "I would like to discuss your latest offer. I suggest you accompany me back to my palace. My chef will have luncheon prepared, and we can discuss matters in comfort."

*At your palace.* Nigella almost giggled. It sounded so absurd. Or was this really about getting her off Adjalane land?

She wasn't convinced this was the best path to the sea. If the ground proved too rocky, costs would soar. Or would they have to do an above-ground pipeline and what kind of exposure to terrorists would that create? She had a hundred questions about this deal—and she wasn't sure if Malid Adjalane's job was to sell her on a hunk of useless land, or was he here to fleece her for a ridiculous amount of money?

One dark eyebrow lifted over his dark sunglasses. Again, she wanted to see his eyes, and she might get a chance over lunch. She called out to her guys to pack it up for now. She turned to tell Malid she'd follow him to his...palace.

But Malid was waving to the guy who'd come with him and already had hold of Nigella by the elbow. "Fadin will drive us. Your men may not be able to follow, so they had best return to their hotel."

The guy—Fadin—inclined his head and then spoke briefly with her men. Nigella stiffened at that bit of high-handed take over—they were her men. But she didn't need to get into a battle this early in the game.

Malid opened the door for her, and she slid into the back seat. "Nice ride," she told him.

"More dependable in the desert." Fadin slipped into the driver's seat and started the engine. Air conditioning stirred cool air over her skin. The car smelled of leather and money.

She eyed Malid, who was slipping into the seat next to her. "You don't have to sit back here with me," she informed him.

He offered another of those charming smiles that he seemed to use so well. "But I want to. Now, what shall we talk of on the ride there?"

# Chapter 2

"Your home is lovely," Nigella said. And it was. They'd driven through a gated entrance into a courtyard. Palm trees, lush foliage, flowering plants, and fountains lined a circular drive. The building—pale sandstone in stark, modern lines—seemed almost a backdrop to the garden. On the drive over, they'd talked about Al-Sarid's history—it's struggle to hold onto its independence and not be swallowed up by other, larger or richer countries, and its efforts to modernize and adapt to a parliamentary form of government. Nigella came away with the clear impression that families such as the Adjalane were still informal rulers who influenced everything. She was going to have to be careful when dealing with them.

Malid held out his hand to help her from the SUV. He gestured to the high walls and the very solid gate. "We are in sandstorm season, and so an interior entrance from the garage as well as this one, and walls are most useful to block most of the sand. Fadin, please tell the kitchen we will be having luncheon on the second floor balcony." He glanced back to her and asked, "Do you like nature?"

She ignored the hand held out to her and used the excuse of gawking to climb out on her own. She turned in a circle. "Back in Texas we have a greenhouse—it's my retreat. The mansion's big and the ranch is even bigger, and growing up that greenhouse was Tarzan's jungle, and I was Indiana Jones."

Malid laughed—he actually laughed. She turned and saw he'd pulled off his sunglasses—at last. His dark eyes gleamed with amusement, and she started to think this deal wouldn't be that hard to pull off. "You are mixing your fiction," Malid told her.

She grinned. "Oh, always."

Taking her arm, he led her inside. Short of being rude and pulling away, she didn't know how to get his hands off her, but maybe she shouldn't try so hard. *He's just being polite*, she told herself. But she also gave a small shiver. She liked those strong wrists and long fingers on her skin just a touch too much.

She also found herself liking the clean lines inside. Not quite stark, but modern and sparse, with a vibrant use of colors—dark blues, reds, orange and yellows—in the artwork choices which were all excellent, modern works, the carpets, which looked old and richly worked, and thick drapery that bracketed sheer linen.

Malid led her upstairs and to a balcony where a dining table of glass and wrought iron had been set up. He gestured toward one of the chairs, and she seated herself.

"Your name...it seems unusual," he asked. He took the chair opposite her. She relaxed back against the thick cushions. It wasn't too personal a question, but it was an ice breaker, and one she was used to.

A young woman in a very modern maid's uniform came out of the house and filled water glasses for them. Nigella sipped and said, "Gordon Michaels was hoping for a son—Nigel was going to be his name."

"And he got you instead?"

She nodded. "But Daddy likes to stick to a plan. So I got the name—only a little adjusted."

"And now you're following his footsteps?"

She smiled. "I'm Daddy's problem solver." And his deal maker. She'd learned young how to twist arms, leverage weaknesses and bargain hard. This, however, was due to be the longest pipeline in the Middle East and the crowning jewel in Opell Oil's empire. Gordon had made her work hard to get her hands on this deal—and he'd all but said he was now looking at her to run the company when he retired at the end of the year.

But that wasn't certain yet.

Gordon had two others—Benson and Williams—that he'd also been grooming for top spots, and Nigella knew that when it came to business, Gordon put the company ahead of family. The way it should be. Of course, that still stung at times. Which meant she was going to earn the right to take over from Daddy—and this deal would prove her worthy. Yet again.

She glanced out at the courtyard they were overlooking, and blinked hard. She wasn't going to dig up old wounds—not the ones that had her having to work harder than any son. She was here to prove to Daddy that she had what it took to be the next head of Opell Oil.

Waving her water glass, she asked, "So…did you buy or build all this?"

Malid shook his head. He sat back, hands folded over a very flat stomach. He'd taken off his ball cap and had dragged his fingers through his hair, leaving it disordered. She almost wanted to do the same thing. Thankfully, the maid came back with two others—and plates with salads, the hummus she'd learned you always got anywhere in the Middle East, flatbread, fruits, something that smelled like roast lamb, and finely chopped cucumbers mixed with olives. She realized she was hungry and started to help herself.

Malid sipped his water and gave her that mysterious smile of his. "Not quite. Now, before you ruin our luncheon by asking more questions that will no doubt lead to a subject I despise, I suggest we discuss the details of your offer."

She raised an eyebrow in his direction and dug into the flatbread. It was fresh, melted in her mouth, and was perfect. She nodded and pulled out a sheaf of papers from her messenger bag. In the field, she liked to have hard copy, not computers. "That's the offer my father presented to your father."

Malid took the papers and read through them. Nigella shamelessly ate. The lamb was as good as the smell promised—moist, marinated in something with citrus and delicately spiced. The fruits were perfectly ripe and sweet. She could get used to this diet. Then Malid started to frown, and Nigella's stomach tightened. He glanced at her. "Opell Oil wants to purchase the land, not just lease it? You expect us to sell land that has been in our family for over two centuries?"

Putting down the flatbread—the meal was to be eaten with the fingers, her favorite kind of food—Nigella wiped her hands on her napkin and met that dark-eyed, steady gaze. The man would make a great poker player, and she had thought this might be an issue that would need to be hammered out. "I've done a comparable cost analysis for similar land, and I believe our offer is more than fair. Do you see a problem?"

Eyes narrowing, he put the papers down on the table. "Adjalane will not sell you the land."

She let out a breath. "We are looking at other sites. A long-term lease is just…well, it means we would build a resource that would one day not be ours, and we like to look at the long term."

That damn smile came out again—it was starting to torment her. "Come up with another offer."

Nigella picked up her water. Okay, so he was going to play hardball. She could do that. "I'll have to give it some thought."

"No, right here. Right now. Surely you can come up with a counter that I will find more appealing?"

Frowning, she wanted to pick up an olive and throw it at him. That was childish. Instead, she put down her water and smiled back. "I'll have to look at the numbers again. And we'll want to look at those other sites first."

Malid shook his head and made a tsking noise that had her clenching her hand around her napkin. "Do you take your time with all major decisions?" he asked.

"I find it makes for fewer mistakes and not so many regrets. Due diligence is not a bad thing." Daddy might love to act from his gut. She didn't. Given that Malid had done something to get himself booted from the family, she was betting he had his own hot temper.

She held Malid's gaze, daring him to challenge her decision-making process. He just smiled back, those lush lips curved with a secret. "You've never known the adrenaline rush of making a split second decision and living with the consequences, be they good or bad?"

"I don't like surprises." She let the words out in a flat tone. It was about time he learned she wasn't going to be swayed.

Just as fast, the smile went to a blaze that took her breath. He swept out a hand. "Let us forget about business and enjoy our meal." He dug into the food, started asking if she had any hobbies, spoke of places he had seen in his travels and asked if she traveled much.

She had, but she was still suspicious of this sudden shift. "Daddy was in the air more than he was on the ground, and with my mother's passing, he started taking me with him. That and the nanny of the week got me to college. Daddy's a demanding individual, and not many of the hired help ever could put up with him for more than a few months."

"Did you not grow tired of the constant change?" Malid asked. He leaned forward. "I ask, having had the same caretakers my entire life."

She had to smile at that. "Makes you adept at getting people to do what you want them to, doesn't it?"

He offered her more flatbread. She was tempted, but had to decline—she'd been pigging out on the hummus. Malid helped himself and said, "My guess is you are very good at what you do."

"Fishing there?" He gave her a blank look, and she said, "It's called catching more flies with honey than you do with vinegar, and you're spreading the sweet on a tad too thick there."

"I will keep that in mind as we go forward in business then."

***

After lunch, Malid suggested a walk through the gardens. Nigella agreed. They kept to safe topics—Nigella was interested in what would grow in the heat, and Malid talked of irrigation and shading.

It seemed to him that a chemistry simmered between them, but he did not know yet what to make of that. Would it be useful—or a distraction? Nigella was certainly a pleasant visual that kept snagging his stare as she bent to sniff at the jasmine or turned to admire one of the many fountains that helped to cool the courtyard and the house. He liked her long legs, the way she moved—he even liked the touch of a drawl that slipped into her words when she spoke of home.

She seemed, too, to approve of his palace.

The doors stood open on the ground floor and sheer, white drapery billowed out from the rooms. The splash of the fountains also made for a pleasant background sound. He plucked a hibiscus—a vivid red bloom and presented it to her. Her cheeks pinked, but she seemed not to care for a great deal of flattery.

A blunt woman, he thought. Refreshingly so. But quite as determined to get her way as he was. He would take his time with this deal, he decided. There was chemistry between them—they were alike in some things, he thought, and that intrigued him. But business was business, and he could not let an attraction make him stupid. One thing he had learned over the past few months was the value of patience—and he was determined to see Nigella be the one to give on the matter of this lease.

# Chapter 3

Malid sent Nigella home in his car—Fadin would drive her back to her hotel. He thought about going along—it was a two-hour drive and he wanted to spend more time with her, to figure her out. But Nigella was starting to look decided jet lagged. And she had said she needed time to think.

He agreed to meet her at the temporary headquarters for Opell Oil in two days. Malid planned to use the time to find out more about her and any possible weaknesses in Opell Oil. It was possible he could structure a price that would make a lease far more appealing to her and her father.

Watching the car pull away, Malid wondered if such a woman as her had a husband. He did not think so. She wore no ring, and she had the air of someone whose life had been consumed by business. He knew about that, too. Until he had earned his father's disapproval, Malid's life and ambition had been to be the CEO of the family's company. Now...now he had more time on his hands than he knew what to do with.

He had started a few small companies—technology ventures, which would encourage young people to stay in Al-Sarid, and a few charities that could help some of the nomadic tribes deal with the ever-changing world. He had grown tired of any kind of night clubbing years ago—and in some ways he thought it a pity he had never married. A family would have been a good distraction for him. But he had never had time before now.

Perhaps he was more like Nigella in that way—both of them consumed by business, by making the deal, by being the best.

He headed back inside the palace, thinking of her and her expressive, amethyst eyes.

*** 

Malid stepped out of the vehicle, grateful that Fadin had insisted on driving him to this meeting with Nigella. It gave him extra time to think of possible tactics he might have to use and to catch up with his other ventures, which he had neglected over the past two days.

He had kept himself busy digging into Opell Oil. Given how oil prices had not been good of late—rising and falling and being utterly undependable—the company was looking to diversify. They had been quietly investing into other technologies—wind and solar power among them. That could be useful for Al-Sarid and another way to encourage Opell to seek a lease—with options for solar and wind installations.

He'd also received word from one of his sources that Opell Oil had been speaking with officials in the neighboring country of Tawzar, which was eager to get the Opell pipeline.

Tawzar had struggled to keep up with both newer technology and oil production. He knew they could greatly use the revenues from such a deal, and that might lead them to attempt giving Opell far more than the Adjalane family intended to offer. However, Tawzar had an unstable government—that was the greatest drawback. Malid would use that if he needed to, but he hoped he could secure a deal with Nigella today without mention of Tawzar.

Opell Oil had set up temporary offices in a high rise that blended technology with old world charm of the coastal city in Dubai. It was interesting they had not chosen to lease space in Al-Sarid. He did not believe in signs and omens—but he did believe in the unspoken message. This message clearly said that Opell Oil had not yet fixed on Al-Sarid as their best option for a pipeline.

In the lobby, Malid noted that Opell Oil had offices on the thirty-fifth floor. He enjoyed the view of the city as the glass-enclosed elevator carried him upward.

Nigella would hopefully have another offer—if she didn't, he had several ideas to present for her consideration. The idea of seeing her again sent a pleasant shiver over his skin. He was moderately curious to see if the attraction he'd felt between them the other day remained or had it been a passing fancy—an interest only because she had seemed so different from the other women he had met over his life.

Stepping out of the elevator, he took in thick, slate-colored carpets, a floral arrangement on a side table, a large piece of slate with water cascading down it, and the opaque walls of glass that provided the occupants inside the offices privacy.

The receptionist seemed to expect him for she showed him into a conference room with a view of Dubai and the sea.

Malid hated to be kept waiting—in his life, people waited on him, not the other way around. However, this was business. Hiding his irritation, he took a seat at the boardroom table. It was large and of a polished mahogany that spoke of money. He, too had dressed to impress—an Armani suit and tie, with a white *taub* over it and the *keffiyeh* favored by his family. Today, he was Sheikh Malid Adjalane. Anyone who saw him in traditional robes would know he was a person of importance and authority.

Staring out at the skyline, he wondered what Nigella would think of his garb—and what would she be wearing?

The snick of a door opening behind him had him turning, but Nigella brought another man with her. The resemblance was obvious at once

Gordon Michaels had the same eyes as his daughter, the same dark hair—almost black with a touch of brown. However, gray streaked his hair. Age, sun and weather had lined his skin. He obviously kept himself fit—but Malid was going to guess he had been ill recently. Instead of his coat being a perfect fit, it hung a touch loose. He came into the room, and Malid stood—the man's personality was such that he swept in with arrogance and domination. Malid stiffened and glanced at Nigella.

She'd dressed in a black business suit—a thin skirt, a silk button-down blouse, a blazer over the top. Her hair was pulled back, and her makeup was as bold as her jewelry today. Judging by her expression, she was not happy to have her father with her today.

Malid turned to Gordon Michaels. "I assumed I would be meeting with your daughter."

The other man didn't even look at Nigella. It was as if she wasn't even in the room. He glanced at Malid's robes and said, "What seems to be the problem with my offer?"

Glancing at Nigella, Malid lifted an eyebrow. She dropped her stare to the floor—ah, so she could do nothing with her father. He knew the feeling. Turning back to Michaels, he said, "Nigella called you? Or emailed? And you think somehow you must fly here and fix this in person—that she was not able to handle this?"

Michaels huffed out a breath. "You trying to hold my company hostage? We put a huge sum on the table for what amounts to little more than piles of sand."

"Daddy—?"

Michaels slashed his hand, silencing Nigella. Her cheeks pinked, and Malid's face heated. This was a family matter obviously, but Michaels was pulling Malid into it. He forced himself to smile and sit down. "I came here to negotiate with Nigella—not you."

Crossing his arms, Michaels said, "If I have to, we'll go east and run the pipeline through Tawzar. And you and your backwards country can go on still livin' in the dark ages."

Nigella stepped forward, pushing between her father and Malid. "Daddy—can we have a word?"

Glancing from Nigella to her father, Malid wondered who would win this contest of wills between them. Until now, Nigella had seemed unable to do much with her father—now, however, now she looked a spitfire. A warrior ready to do battle. In heels, she stood as tall as her father—and she looked him in the eye. Michaels hesitated—and Nigella used that moment. She put a hand on his arm and her drawl thickened. "Please, Daddy."

What man could resist that tone? Malid saw Michaels soften—the man's eyes lost their sharp edge, his shoulders eased and he gave a quick nod. He shot a last look at Malid as if to promise this wasn't settled yet, but he let his daughter lead him from the conference room, mild as a lamb.

And wasn't that interesting.

It seemed there was an unofficial power struggle within the Opell Oil. In his research, Malid had read that Gordon Michaels was grooming possible successors. There had not been a word about any illness—but the man he had just met was not the same, robust man he had seen in so many images online. This put a new slant on things. Opell Oil might need this pipeline sooner than Malid had thought— if Michaels died while he was still CEO, Opell Oil stock would drop. That was only to be expected. It would no doubt recover—but the company would be exposed to hostile takeovers. Michaels would be wise to name a successor and ensure a smooth transition that would leave stockholders feeling secure enough that they did not rush to sell their shares

That meant Nigella Michaels would no doubt want to secure the pipeline at once.

Malid smiled—suddenly he knew it was in his best interests to drag out negotiations. Opell Oil would soon be begging to sign any deal. All he must do is distract Nigella and keep the deal in play just long enough.

# Chapter 4

Nigella stepped back into the conference room. It had taken coaxing her daddy, badgering him, reminding him what the doctor had said about his blood pressure, and then reminding him that he'd promised her she'd be lead on this deal. That had finally done it. Gordon Michaels might be a tough, stubborn son-of-a-bitch, but his word and handshake were legendary—as solid as gold in the bank. She'd outlined how she planned to go at Malid, and he'd finally agreed that her tactics were good.

She'd also gotten him to admit he didn't understand the culture of the region, nor did he want to. In his mind, the universal language was dollars. She'd told him time and again that family and heritage often trumped monetary gain. He'd never gotten that message—but he had agreed she was still his problem solver.

And Malid was proving to be a problem.

Smiling at him, she came over to him. She'd left him sitting in one of the chairs, but now he was standing. He'd been staring out the floor-to-ceiling windows when she'd entered, but he'd turned.

"I apologize for my father—he's…well, he just flew in and he's never in the best mood after a long flight. If you'll come with me, we can finish our meeting in my office. I can promise you there will be no more interference from Daddy. He's got…well, he's actually here on a different matter." Searching Malid's dark eyes—they looked hard and cold just now—she tried to convey how sorry she was and silently begged him to give her the chance she was asking for.

He inclined his head. "I must admit I, too, know what it is to be at odds with one's father. It is the one good thing of being asked to absent myself—while I have missed my home and certain members of my family, I haven't missed fighting with Nimr. And the approved way for my brothers Adilan and Nassir and I to settle an argument is with fists. That I haven't missed, either."

The knot loosened in her stomach. "Well, Daddy's not much of one for punching, but he did teach me to box when I was twelve." Turning, she led the way down the hall and to her corner office. A few days and she'd already turned it into her space—meaning lots of mess. Papers cluttered the rosewood desk, books spilled from the shelves, and the only feminine touch she'd allowed herself was an exotic carpet, locally made and antique. She loved the rose and tan hues in the carpet and had bought it despite the ridiculous price charged. This was her space now—and she firmly shut the door.

Malid walked to the large wall of windows behind her desk. She had a silver tea set on a table near an overstuffed sofa, but he ignored comfort for the view. "This city is amazing—I never tire of visiting."

Joining him, Nigella folded her arms. She made sure to stand a few feet away. He looked even more the dashing sheikh today, with his robes and the headscarf she'd seen on other men. He also smelled good—like sandalwood or something else exotic and spicy. For some reason, she'd thought he'd show up in a suit—and he had. But the addition of the traditional clothing left him…well, looking very much a prince of the desert.

She'd tried to pound that part of it into Daddy's head—
the Adjalane family was just about royalty in these parts.
But Daddy was a Texas son through and through—it
wasn't so much that he believed all men were created
equal as he thought princes were something that belonged
in story books.

Giving a nod to the view spread out below them—blue
water and high rises all sparkling in the sunlight—she said,
"Your part of the world is beautiful in such unexpected
ways."

Malid nodded and turned to face her. "You are quite
certain your father has agreed to let you handle the
negotiations from here on out?"

"Daddy had a point. Tawzar is an option—I'm not
taking it off the table. But I'd like to think there's some
way we can work out a deal with your family that makes
everyone happy."

He seemed to consider the idea. Nigella held her breath.
She hoped Malid hadn't figured out that Tawzar was a last
resort for Opall Oil—the place was notoriously unstable
and she didn't see that changing in the future. Daddy might

think the good old US of A would come in guns blazing to help protect a U.S. company, but Nigella would prefer dealing with a stable country.

Stepping over to her desk, Nigella spread out some photos. "I flew over Tawzar yesterday by helicopter. It was barren, but I could see some good potential spots for a pipeline."

"What did you say about vinegar and honey? Is it not vinegar to talk of Tawzar? And you would have to add thousands of miles of pipe. Have you done the same...fly over with Al-Sarid?"

She shook her head. Did he have to stand so dang close. She could feel the heat of his body and smell that teasing spicy scent. "The piece we saw a few days ago was all I've seen." Pressing a hand to her stomach, which was already rolling at the thought of another helicopter ride, she admitted, "Have to say, I did not enjoy all that dipping and diving. Not at all."

Malid smiled. "There is so much more to see in Al-Sarid. And better ways to see it. What are you doing for the rest of the day?"

Nigella cocked her head to one side. Just what was he planning here? "My calendar's clear. I wasn't sure how long our meeting would take."

"Then let me show you my country. Let me prove to you why Al-Sarid is the perfect place for your pipeline, and also show you why a lease would ally you to my family, which would be of greater benefit to Opell Oil. I promise we will not be taking any helicopters. What I have in mind is something much more…traditional. Old school, if you will."

"Don't tell me—camels?"

Malid lifted a hand. "For part of the journey. Clear your calendar for tomorrow as well—and the day after" He offered up a boyish grin. Her stomach gave a flip. Damn, but when he wanted to put on the charm it came out hot as the sun in the desert. She couldn't help but stare at him like she was fourteen with her first crush—those amazing, dark eyes, and those lush lips that curved right now and looked all too inviting.

Heat tingled on her cheeks. And what was she thinking? Three days with him in the desert? Why would that be so bad?

She knew the dangers of mixing business with pleasure. She'd had one office fling, had it go sour, and had to endure seeing the guy for another six months as he charmed his way around through half a dozen more affairs. HR had finally booted the guy for sexual harassment.

But Malid—this was a deal that would be done, and if getting him in bed got the deal done faster, nothing wrong with that.

She smiled back at him. "Don't tell me you're going for the cliché of a sheikh who carries a woman off to his desert tent?"

Malid stepped closer. "We leave in fifteen minutes."

She gave a laugh then realized he was serious. Shaking her head, she told him, "I can't possibly be ready by then."

"I will have everything you need waiting for us when we reach the border. What use is my carrying you off if I can't...well, carry you off." He tapped one finger on her cheek. "I promise you will not regret anything."

Nigella pressed her lips tight. She never acted without looking at things from all sides. Never. Going away like this was not something she'd ever done—or did. She'd dated plenty, but it was always with a plan and a schedule and a...and boy had those all worked out badly.

She sucked in a breath and let it out. It was not how she operated and this was so far outside her comfort zone, it took everything within her to actually nod at him and give him a smile.

***

Malid strode from the room and was already on the phone by the time he stepped into the elevator. Arrangements would need to be made, but this gave him an excellent reason to return to Al-Sarid. After speaking to Fadin about what was needed, he called his father's private line.

"Malid, I assume you are calling to say the deal is made?" Nimr sounded tired—exhausted in fact.

Malid pushed down the urge to ask about that. His father would admit to nothing, and that was not the purpose of this call. "I need to bring Michaels into Al-Sarid." He intentionally did not say which Michaels. "I need a few days."

Silence stretched out, and then Nimr said, "Very well. I will ensure you are not bothered."

Wetting his lips, Malid wondered what else he should say. He could think of nothing, so he asked, "How is she? How is mother?" He smoothed his tie. He felt like cursing his father, but he had to admit he had brought this on himself. He had been the one who had wanted Al-Hilah back at any cost. Bitterness rose in his throat. He pulled in a breath and said, "Give mother my best and tell her I will see her shortly." He cut off the call before Nimr could.

Outside, Fadin stood waiting next to the SUV. "Everything you asked for is in order. Did you speak with your father to clear the path?"

"I did." Malid stuffed his hands into his pockets. "That man would keep me from seeing my mother before she dies."

"Are you so sure she is that ill? Nimr, as you know better than most, is a master at deception—who else taught you to lie if you must, so long as you do not lose control?"

Malid frowned. Had his father really taught him that? Or was that something he had learned on his own? As the eldest of three boys, Malid had grown up competing for attention—to be the best. It had become an obsession, Malid knew, and now he wondered if perhaps he had learned the wrong lessons from his father. He shook his head. "I cannot lose focus. Gordon Michaels decided to come look over his daughter's shoulder—and he is an American version of my father—arrogant, stubborn, certain his way is the only way." A grin spread across Fadin's face, and Malid demanded, "Why do you smile?"

"Forgive me, but it sounds as if you describe yourself. And now…what are you going to do with this American woman for three days?"

Malid smiled. "I am going to drag out negotiations until I get what I want, of course."

# Chapter 5

Nigella was having the time of her life. Malid had taken care of everything, food—they ate a lovely picnic lunch on the road—water, and traditional clothing waiting for her when they reached the border of Al-Sarid. From there, they had driven for well over an hour before coming to a small, Bedouin encampment where several tents had been set up. Malid spoke to the nomads, and then told Nigella he had asked the two women to accompany Nigella and help her figure out traditional dress.

"It may seem strange to you, but I promise you will be more comfortable," he'd told her.

She'd been amused, and had jokingly whispered to him that he could have helped her. His response still echoed in her ears. "Nigella, when I help you remove your clothing, it will not be to immediately put different ones back on your person."

Face hot, she'd hurried into the tent, grateful the women helping her hadn't understood any of the English—or so she hoped. The Bedouin in their black robes helped her remove her clothing, insisting she also remove her undergarments with their gestures and fast Arabic. She had tried to wave them off, but the older of the two women had scolded her in terms that were clear in any language and pushed the clothes into Nigella's hands.

Reluctantly, Nigella had taken the light, cotton garments and quickly changed. The cropped shift and a pair of boy's briefs hung loosely on her, and were immediately cooler than her western underwear. She would need to do some shopping if she was going to spend more time in this region.

They handed her a thin pair of loose trousers, a long-sleeve shirt of lightweight linen and several other layers. She had thought the black robes would be heavy and hot, but instead they seemed light and somehow managed to catch any breeze and allow it to slip onto her skin. Finally, they insisted she done a head scarf. She tried to resist, but the women wouldn't let her out without the scarf. When it was done, the two women giggled and clapped their hands, then threw back the tent flap and gestured for her to follow. Nigella wondered what Malid would think of her new look.

She stepped from the tent, and he turned, his eyes brightening. He took her hand. "You are more beautiful than I could have hoped for."

"Thank you. You don't look so bad yourself."

Malid had changed as well, into the black tunic, loose trousers and robes of a nomad. The scarf that covered his head fell down to his waist. He tugged at her head scarf, arranging the folds of fabric around her shoulders and told her, "The length of the sides can be used to shield your face and mouth should it become necessary in case of sandstorms. We are going to be travelling by camel. Keep your hands and face covered as much as possible to shield your skin."

The three Bedouin men led two, single-humped camels to them, and Nigella slipped a little bit behind Malid. The animals seemed dangerously tall and didn't look at all friendly. "I've heard they spit," she said.

Malid grinned. "Yes. So don't stand in front of them. They also have terrible breath and can go for days without water. Is there a problem?"

She didn't want to ruin the excursion, but common sense and self-preservation had gone to high alert. "I don't think I can ride one of those things by myself."

"Of course you can. But would you feel better if we rode tandem?"

Relief swept into her. It would be just her luck to get the bad-tempered beast and have it run off with her. If Malid was driving, she was not going to end up looking like a silly, screaming girl.

Malid turned and gave instructions to the camel handlers, who shrugged and swapped saddles.

Several satchels were fasted to the second camel, and when Nigella asked about that, Malid told her, "Supplies. I intend for us to reach our destination around dusk, but one never travels in the desert without survival in mind."

"Uh, maybe we should just take a vehicle?"

"Nonsense. Wheels more easily become stuck in sand. And I want you to experience my country in all of its glory. This is the best way to do that—you cannot know the land without becoming one with nature. Now, let me assist you up and I will follow."

Malid tapped the camel's front leg. It let out a donkey-like bray but went down on its knees and lay down. The camel had rich, long lashes over big, dark eyes, but Nigella wasn't fooled. The beast was chewing something and kept giving her sideways glances, as if just looking for an opportunity to purse its thick lips and spit at her.

She scrambled onto the saddle, which seemed more like a large pillow with a wooden frame and railings, or a sideways couch. Malid climbed up behind her, pulling her back against him to sit in the cradle of his thighs. She could smell the spicy cologne he used, and a hint of pure, male musk. Her pulse kicked up and she started rethinking the wisdom of this adventure—but she was committed.

"Relax," he said, and his breath brushed her cheek. "I'll keep you safe." He tapped the camel again with the long stick that seemed made for this purpose. It rose—front first then the hind end coming up. Nigella clung to the wood in front of her. Her heart was pounding now, and she swallowed hard. She did not want to look weak, but right now that helicopter was sounding pretty good.

Malid took up the reins in one hand and wrapped his other arm around her waist. "Hold on." Suddenly, everything was shifting, and the camel was moving, and Nigella wondered if she could possibly turn and simply bury her face in Malid's broad chest. Instead she closed her eyes and the camel lurched forward into a bouncing trot.

\*\*\*

Malid could feel the tension in Nigella's slim shoulders. Gradually, it eased. The Bedouin encampment became a dot on the horizon and the desert began to work its magic. The sounds of the city had long ago vanished. The distant cry of a hawk hunting a meal carried to them. A light breeze brought the dry smells of the desert plants—faint aromas that promised an oasis ahead. The mountains—purple and jagged—rose before them, still distant but in the desert one could see for miles. The ground shifted from rocky to sandy, but Malid knew this track well, even though it was poorly marked.

This was his homeland, and it was as beautiful as it was dangerous, which was probably why it appealed so much to him. The rocking gait of the camel meant Nigella had to lean against him—he liked the motion, and the feel of her body against his. In general, he did not care to mix business with complications—however, Nigella seemed to him an exception to any rule. The truth was he wanted her—and he saw no reason they could not make the next few days a pleasure. And she might also then be more willing to make a deal that pleased him fully.

Leaning forward, he asked Nigella. "Well, what do you think?"

Nigella turned her head slightly and met his eyes. "This is all...just—"

"New? Exciting? Exhilarating?" Malid gave her a grin. "You smell as sweet as an oasis, you know." He used the arm around her waist to pull her closer to himself. "Look to your left."

A plateau rose up from the small rolling hills around them. "There are many parts of the desert that are nothing but dunes, but in this part of Al-Sarid, the land varies."

"How do you navigate all this?" She waved a hand at the open space around them—at the rocks and sands and distant hills.

"You should learn land marks—that plateau, the sun's position, where the moon rises. The day's heat is fading and the stars will help as well."

"Just where are we headed? I mean, we're not going to spend the night under the stars, are we?" Nigella asked.

He heard the slight quiver in her voice and frowned. "What—you would miss having a bed and a four-star hotel?"

"It's just…well, okay, I have to admit I ended up getting lost in Jamaica for a couple of days."

He gave a laugh. "That doesn't sound a hardship."

She stiffened and slanted a glare at him. "It is if it's jungle, wet, horribly humid with very large bugs. I'm still sure some kind of big cat was looking to make a meal of me."

"And where was your father?" Malid asked. "Hunting for you and worried?"

Nigella let out a breath that was more of sigh. "In negotiations. He was trying to mix a vacation for me with work, and my nanny at the time quit without notice. I got bored and started chasing butterflies and succeeded in getting utterly lost."

"Ah, then you should like the desert. The sky is always visible and can always guide you safely. But since you have told me your dark secret, I will tell you mine—my father intentionally took me into the desert when I was eight to teach me the old ways, and on the fourth morning I woke to find myself alone with a tent, two skins of water and a knife."

Nigella turned halfway around to face him. "Oh, my god—how long were you out there?"

"Three of the longest days of my life. But I never forgot the lessons I learned during those three days—never to trust my father again and that I could handle whatever was thrown at me. The desert became my sanctuary."

She shifted in the saddle, her hips rubbing against him in a distracting way. He glanced at her, but she was staring out at the horizon now, where the sun was starting to dip behind the mountains. "Myself, I was left with a profound desire to stay far from any jungle. That's a huge advantage you have here. And is that…okay, is that a real oasis or a desert mirage."

He leaned closer. "That, Nigella, is one of the many blessings of Al-Sarid. We have springs across much of the land—including several that would be near where your pipeline would be built. These are what make travel in Al-Sarid possible."

The camel seemed to know they were nearing water, for it quickened its speed. Malid let the camel—and the second one whose reins were tied to back of the saddle—pick up speed. As per his orders, tents had been made ready for their arrival. An older man in traditional garb, but in loose white robes—met them, taking charge of the camels and unloading their supplies.

Malid offered up greetings, and he could smell a meal cooking. Malid turned to escort Nigella to their tent, only to find that she had wandered off. She was ambling around the spring that watered the date palms here and the grasses.

He followed her, watching as she gently touched a flower petal, and bent to smell their fragrance.

She must have heard his boots on the sand, for she turned and smiled. "This place is like paradise. Why would you ever leave here to live in a city?"

Malid shook his head. "You are seeing it at the perfect time of day—with the cool of evening and a full moon. But in sandstorm season, it is not so pleasant." He took her hand. "Now, do you want to stay to admire the night or would you prefer to dine?"

# Chapter 6

Dinner was amazing—lamb and goat roasted over a fire. Dates, honey, and vegetables mixed with spices and cooked in a clay pot. Flatbread still warm from baking. Malid insisted on feeding her small bites of everything, and smiled when her lips or tongue would touch his fingers. They ate with their hands—after washing with water poured from a metal pitcher into a metal basin. Afterwards, mint tea was brewed and served—strong and sweet.

They'd eaten outside the main tent, sitting on pillows on a thick, wool carpet that gave the setting a sense of decadence. Nigella had eaten at the best restaurants in New York and across all of Europe. She'd been to Texas barbeques where sides of beef were severed on platters that you had to hold with two hands with beans and cornbread. But never had anything tasted as good as food from Malid's fingers. She hadn't had a drop of alcohol, but she felt tipsy just on the experience.

As the night fell, turning the sky a deep purple with stars spread over the darkness in a wash of light, Malid pointed out the various constellations and cardinal navigation points. She decided she could listen to that deep, sexy voice of his all night.

And then he asked, "Would you care for a swim in the oasis?"

She glanced at him. "You're kidding, right?"

"That is the best bath you will have. Won't it feel good to rinse away the sweat of the day?"

She looked over to the darkness of the water. A fire burned in front of them within a circle of rocks, but beyond the small glow of bright flame, the night seemed almost black. The others who had prepared dinner and waited on them had gone into one of the smaller tents, and Nigella could hear the quite hum of conversation in Arabic, and someone seemed to be tuning a stringed instrument. She glanced again at Malid. "We'll, I used to go skinny-dipping back in Texas. I suppose this won't be much different."

His mouth quirked up. "How can you skinny dip if you are not skinny—and a dip is not a swim."

She stood, and he did as well. He seemed to have cat's eyes—she stumbled over a rock and he took her hand and led her to the pool of spring water. Sitting down, she pulled off her boots and dipped a toe in the water—it was surprisingly warm, holding the heat of the day still. She glanced at Malid. "Are there fish in there? Snakes?"

"I assure it. It is utterly safe." He pulled off his vest and tunic—moonlight glinted on his smooth chest and arms. Nigella's mouth went dry.

Okay, so he was better than any fantasy sheikh. He kept himself in great physical condition, so he must workout. She wanted to put a hand on those lean muscles, to trail her fingers down that smooth skin. It wasn't just his arrogance that drew her to him—she knew she had Daddy issues, since she was drawn to strong men with way too much cocky confidence. But Malid had another side.

He'd shared a story that he didn't have to about being left in the desert, and that was just to make her feel better about her having admitted a weakness. He had brains—this was a smooth move; she knew to seduce her into falling in love with Al-Sarid. She could admire that. He had charm and he used it—but he also had the loyalty of his people. She'd caught small glances between those who served him and she'd also was catching on that he was a guy who always remembered to say thank you.

She was drawn to him in ways she hadn't been to any man—that both worried her a little and sent pleasure shooting down her spine.

Malid was starting to strip off his boots and pants, and Nigella began to feel overdressed. She stood and stripped down to her borrowed underwear. She was tempted to go swimming in just that, but—well, what the hell. How often did a girl get her own sheikh at a desert oasis?

Shucking the last of her clothes, she waded into the springs.

The edge was rocky enough to give her some footing. She dipped down into the water. It wasn't that deep—maybe four feet, she thought. Not enough to let you swim. The water lapped warm over her skin, contrasting with the cooling night air.

Naked, Malid walked into the springs. He wasn't something of marble and perfection. She could see a scar on his shoulder and another across his right forearm. Those small marks only seemed to make the rest of him seem better—magnificent was the word that sprang to mind. He didn't have much hair on his chest—just a little low on his belly. He was half-hard—and she liked the size of him. She also liked the smooth muscles.

Reaching out, she touched her fingers to his shoulders. It seemed to be all the invitation he needed.

He wrapped an arm around her waist and pulled her toward him. His hands seemed huge and warm. Her breasts pressed against his hard, warm chest. She gasped, smiled and wrapped her arms around his neck. "This going to be a problem?"

He dipped his head and kissed her, ravaging her mouth. This was no gentle first kiss. He stole her breath, seemed bent on claiming her for the night.

Pulling back, he gave her a chance to drag in some air. His hands moved down her back and over curves of her butt. "What problem do you foresee?"

He pulled her against him. Her thigh brushed against his erection. "Malid, you know perfectly well what."

"You feel so good."

"That is not an answer to anything." She shivered, partly in reaction to the lust swimming through her veins, and partly because the air was getting downright cold. But Malid was warm—no, he was outright hot as a desert sun.

He pulled her closer, kissed the side of her neck and then trailed his mouth down to her breast. She arched, and he reached between them. His fingers brushed over her thigh and settled between her legs.

"This is going to make negotiations complicated." She got the words out with a rushed breath. Pleasure rushed over her skin and sank deeper. She was floating on the water and a haze of Malid's magic.

He gave a hum and helped her to stretch out on the water. "I think negotiations are proceeding quite well—we are…finding a rapport from which we can better reach agreement."

She gave a laugh, and then his mouth settled between her legs. That ended any more discussion. She couldn't talk, couldn't do anything but offer up sighs and try to hang onto his shoulders. She wrapped her fingers in his hair. Overhead, the stars twinkled at her and the black night held them close. She lost herself in the moment—in Malid's clever touch and even more clever tongue. He was doing things to her, making her lose her mind, her sense, her soul.

She came with a gasp and a shiver. Touching his arm, she tried to still his touch. She was shivering now but not from the cold.

"Come," he said. He rose up from the water and held out a hand. She put her fingers into his, and he pulled her from the water. She shivered again—this time in earnest. He grinned. "That is the desert—too hot during the day and too cold at night."

She stepped from the water and grabbed her clothes. Malid already had swept his up. Grinning like a kid, she followed him back to one of the smaller tents. Lanterns had been lit inside, and a small fire burned in what looked like an iron stove or heater. Instant warm spread over her skin. The tent had been hung with carpets and drapery, and more carpets and pillows were piled thick to make a couch or a bed.

Before she could do more than glance around, Malid had her in his arms again. She dropped her clothing and wrapped herself around him, lifting one leg to put it around his calf. "This is not going to change my mind about wanting to buy the land for a pipeline."

One dark eyebrow lifted. "Do you really want to talk business right now?"

She shook her head. He kissed her again. The stubble on his chin brushed her cheek. And then it was all tongue and teeth and passion. He pulled her with him down onto the pillows. She parted her legs, making room for him between them.

Pulling back, he stared at her, his eyes dark and heated. Putting a hand on her breast, he murmured, "Nigella, you are an amazing woman." Bending down, he took one nipple into his mouth and sucked on it.

Letting out a soft moan, she put her hand on his back to urge him to do more. She dug her nails in, then moved her hands to that firm ass of his. She pulled him closer and dug in her fingernails again.

He chuckled and rose up on one elbow. "Someone is in a hurry."

"I'm never in a hurry," she muttered, and kissed and bit his neck.

Malid growled, reached down and pulled her hands away. "Before you completely unman him, enough." He lifted her wrists above her head and pushed them into the pillows." I plan to take my time. You should appreciate that."

"Next time maybe." She tried to pull free, but he held her fast.

"Many more times," he told her and kissed her until she gave up and gave into him.

"Malid, stop teasing," she begged. "It's been so long."

"How long?" he asked, rubbing his erection against her now.

Sweat slicked her skin and she could smell the salty tang of her arousal. "Two years too long."

He brushed a kiss over her breast. "The men in your country are either stupid or blind. Lucky for you, I am neither." Keeping her gaze locked on his own, he reached down and positioned himself at her entrance. "Do we need to think of a condom?" he asked.

She shook her head. "Not unless you've been sleeping with the wrong people or using needles. I protect myself, Malid." She wiggled her hips. "Don't go away on my account. Things were just starting to get interesting."

He slid into her agonizingly slow. "Interesting? Is that the best adjective you can come up with?"

Smiling, she told him, "Why don't you help me come up with some more."

# Chapter 7

Malid pushed deeper into her—Nigella, his Nigella. He shouldn't think of her as such, but he did. She was his now. He wanted to pump his seed into her—to leave a mark on her that would claim her as his. He sank into her, buried himself to the hilt, and held still, savoring the moment.

Her eyes had drifted closed and her skin—that lovely, pale skin—glowed with arousal. Pulling out, he pushed in again—slowly. He wanted to feel every precious inch. She gave a whimper and tugged again on her wrists. Ah, so he had not yet reduced her to being utterly his.

He picked up the pace, pushing in harder now—faster. She gave a moan, and he had to catch a breath and hold still a moment. Her hips bucked up under his and her eyes opened. He could still feel her nails digging into him and he knew how she would like her sex.

Pulling out, he pushed in hard. She gave another moan and buck. He smiled. This was how he liked his sex, too— hard and a little rough. Leaning down, he bit just above her nipple. Bit hard. She wiggled under him and arched. He smiled even more, pulled out and pumped in hard, thrusting so that she would feel his weight and the length of his cock. He wanted to impale her on it—wanted her moaning and trashing beneath him.

He started to pump harder—to take her, to make her his utterly. She wiggled and arched, almost fighting him, but really he knew she was fighting for her own release. Her eyes closed again and he shifted his hips so he could screw her deeper. Setting a faster pace, sweat slicking his skin and hers, he thrust deeper until he could feel himself pushing up against her uterus. She was beautiful like this—hair spilling around her, mouth slack, eyes abandoned to anything but pleasure.

He wanted to see her with her hands tied. He wanted to have her at his mercy. He wanted to blindfold her and drip hot wax on her nipples and watch her writhe as she balanced on that edge between pleasure and pain. He wanted…

Pulling out, he thrust in harder and harder—faster now, gripping her wrists, making her ride the waves of her

orgasm. She gave a cry but that wasn't enough for him—
he wanted to hear that soft almost-sob again. He thrust
harder into her, glad for the firm pillows under her hips,
glad she was a woman built to take a hard ride like this. He
pushed in faster and faster, and now her wrists went limp
under his hold, her body softened. She spread her legs
wider for him, inviting a more punishing ride, and that
inflamed him.

Hips bucking, he rode her, faster and harder—wanting,
always wanting. She gave another cry, softened even more
to him—gave utterly to him—and his own orgasm swept
over him, blurring the world, leaving only the feeling of
being joined utterly to her.

He came back to himself to become aware of the sweat
drying on his skin, his breath slowing, and Nigella under
him. He had loosened her wrists, and now she dragged two
fingers up and down over his arm.

"Spectacular. Blissful. Orgasmic," she muttered, her
voice still drenched with sex. "All of those and more come
to mind."

Rolling off her, he gathered her in his arms. "You still have a mind? I have not done my job."

She gave a low laugh. "Oh, honey, if that's not the heights of passion, then Texas ain't a real state. Mind if I just keep floating?"

Her fingers stilled, and Malid heard a call from outside. He stiffened, listened a moment, and then extracted himself from her arms. "Wait."

Grabbing his trousers, he pulled them on and headed outside. There was no need of more words. He could smell the change in the wind, and sand brushed his cheek. He gave a nod to the man who had called for him, gave orders for the care of the camels, and headed back into the tent to Nigella.

He tossed her the clothes she had discarded earlier. "Get dressed. Quickly." Pulling on his tunic, he reached for his boots.

Nigella slid off the pillows. She looked ravished—her hair rumpled and her face still flushed. But her eyes were alert. "What's wrong?"

"Sandstorm. We need to take shelter."

She glanced around them. "Don't we have shelter here?"

"Quickly, the storm is almost upon us. I will explain, but later."

Thank the heavens, she didn't take time to put everything back on—just the long shift and loose pants. Malid tossed her headdress to her, and she settled it over her tangled hair.

He wrapped his *keffiyeh* around his own head. The flaps of the tent flew open and wind pushed sand inside.

Leaning close to Nigella, he put an arm around her waist and said, "Keep your nose and mouth closed and covered." Pulling her with him, they left the smaller tent. Nigella staggered next to him.

Half blind from the sand, he found his way to the largest tent—the one meant for meals and safely. Inside, he had to push past three layers of carpet and coverings to reach the interior. He glanced around, doing a quick head count. The camels were here, sheltered in a corner, munching grass as if wind was not buffeting the tent like a living thing trying to claw its way inside.

Nigella pressed closed to his side—she wasn't shaking, however. He was proud of her for that. The howls of the wind increased. Malid noticed his people had things well in hand. A fire had been started, mint tea had been set to brew, and the supplies had been brought inside.

Leading Nigella to a pile of pillows, he sat and pulled her down next to him. "We must wait until the wind passes. Close your eyes and try to rest."

She gave him a look as if he was asking the impossible, but she curled up on the pillows. A short time later, he glanced down and saw she had fallen into a light sleep. He brushed the scarf back from her face, and accepted a cup of mint tea. No one spoke much—they were all listening to see if the wind would tear apart the smaller tents, or if it would grow into a monster that might even bring down this tent.

Gradually, the howl softened and lessened. Everyone waited. Malid dozed a little. Daylight began to slip through the tent opening, and everyone began to stir. Leaning over Nigella, Malid touched her shoulder.

Her eyes opened, she sat up and took a shallow breath. "It is safe. I thought the winds would tear everything apart."

"The small tents will have to be checked for damage, but the support beams for this one are sunk deep. It would take a much stronger storm to uproot this tent. That is why everyone took refuge here." Malid tipped her chin up so she had to meet his eyes. "Never go outside during a sandstorm. Ever. The sand can choke you. If you are caught outside, bury yourself against a dune under a rug or next to your camel."

Nigella nodded. "Trust me, that shouldn't be a problem." She yawned and glanced around. "Is that breakfast I smell cooking?" She wrinkled her nose. "Or is it camel."

He grinned. "You are a woman of appetites. Now, after breakfast would you like another swim or to see more of the countryside?"

She smiled. "I had something else in mind."

# Chapter 8

Malid was no longer certain who was seducing whom. Nigella surprised him. While she was cautious when it came to business, in bed she was demanding, adventurous, and he adored the way she softened to his passions. They spent the morning in the tent, the afternoon touring Al-Sarid, covering miles on camel, discussing terms and possibilities. At those times, Nigella was cool and distant, a hard-headed business woman.

At night they dined outside under the stars and retired to the tent. Malid stripped her bare and got his wish to blindfold her eyes and tie her hands and do what he wanted with her. He tormented her with kisses and touches until she was begging for more and he was shaking with need for her, and then he plunged into her, claiming her again.

The next morning over breakfast, Malid hashed out with the terms he could present to his father—Opell Oil would pay an additional twenty percent for the land. Opell Oil would be deeded the land the pipeline sat upon and a buffer of four feet on either side, but if the company should ever abandon the pipeline —which would include stopping production due to leaks, or the sale of its Middle East operations and holdings—the land would revert back to the ownership of the Adjalane's. In addition, Opell Oil would give the Adjalane rights to use the land for eternity, and all water rights on the land would remain with the Adjalane family. Malid sweetened the offer with exclusive rights to negotiate with the Adjalane for additional leases to house wind or solar power operations.

Malid was confident his father would accept those terms. The danger had always been that, at some point, Opell Oil would sell off its Middle East holdings, including any land they had purchased in Al-Sarid.

They shook hands on the deal, and it took all of Malid's will power not to pull Nigella closer for a kiss to seal the deal. The whine of a helicopter, however, interrupted. He stepped outside the tent to see Fadin hunched over as he hurried out from under the blades. When he told Nigella a helicopter had arrived to take them back to the city, she'd smiled but she had also shaken her head.

"Don't get me wrong, it will be great to get back—but…" She glanced around the oasis. "I'm going to miss this."

He nodded. "Life is simple in the desert. If you like, after we sign the deal, perhaps a return to celebrate?"

She was cautious with her answer, neither accepting or denying, and he wondered if this would now become a pleasant memory for both of them. A spurt of anger flared. He squashed it down. He had no claim on her—nor she on him. *But…but what?*

They had shared time and their bodies. They had found pleasure. He had gotten what he wanted. That was the end of this. If she chose not to repeat the experience…well, perhaps she was wise. They came from two different worlds—she was not the docile woman he had thought he would one day marry, and she was obviously married more to her work than to any man.

She changed back into her western clothes—as did Malid—and they left the desert behind. But Malid could not resist one last glance back at the oasis. Did he really wish to leave all they had shared behind?

***

Malid's helicopter landed on his office building in
Dubai. From there, he saw to it that Nigella was driven
back to her hotel. She promised to draw up the papers for
the deal immediately. She'd shaken hands with him
again—and had allowed her hand to linger in his. He
thought he saw something in her eyes—was that regret that
their time was drawing to an end? Or something else?

She left, and he watched the elevator doors close on her.
Turning away, he called his father's private line. When
Nimr answered, Malid said, "I have new terms from
Michaels. I will give them to you when I come to visit my
mother." His father had always been an unyielding man
and Malid had learned that same art of being stubborn at
an early age.

Nimr's voice came back over the phone, calm and firm.
"You may tell me now or not at all."

Malid bit down on his temper. He was tempted to
simply hang up. Let the old man make his own deal. But
this was more about his mother, not about his father. He
would think of her first—and he would remember how

Nigella had been able to keep her emotions firmly in check when it came to business. He took a breath and laid out the terms of the new deal.

"This is a good deal for the family." He knew that if either of his brothers reviewed the deal, they would be more than pleased. Nassir would appreciate the financial advantages and Nassir and Adilan would be happy that water rights had been secured.

Sounding tired, Nimr said, "I am not so old yet that I cannot decide what is a good for the family. I will consider the offer." Nimr hung up, and Malid cursed. He almost threw the phone across the room, but that was childish. His mouth curved as he thought again of Nigella—so abandoned when she wished, and so careful when she needed to be. He put his phone back in his pocket and began to think.

If his mother was as ill as he feared, he could not afford to keep waiting—he would not miss her last moments due to his father's stubborn pride. He had proven to his father that he did not need the man's controlling guidance—he did not need it now.

Pulling out his phone again, he called Fadin. "Ready the car. I'm going to go visit my mother. It is time that he learns that even a tyrant must face limits."

# Chapter 9

He arrived in Al-Sarid without problems—Fadin pulled up in front of the family's palace just outside the main city, and Malid stepped from the SUV. He stopped in the courtyard, his heart tightening—there had been times he had thought he would never see this place again.

Adjalane Palace sat on a slight hill overlooking the city and the sea—it was dark enough, however, that Malid could only see the white towers and not the view of the sea or the distant mountains. The white stone walls gleamed, lit now by spotlights and the moon, the fragrances of the gardens wove around him, stirring old memories of him and his brothers playing here, of his mother tending to the roses she adored and would not allow a gardener to touch, or even of his father in rare smiles as he joined them outside.

Pushing aside the useless emotions stirring, Malid headed for the massive, oak front door.

This deal with Opell Oil had been useful—it had given Malid full access to Al-Sarid again—no one had turned him back at the border or at the palace gates. All he had to do was invoke the magic words that he was here to discuss Opell Oil.

He headed at once for his mother's rooms—but they lay beyond Nimr's study. His father came out of that room and blocked the hallway.

Pausing, Malid studied his father.

Nimr looked as if he had aged a decade—not just a few months. His jaw line sagged now, and his nose seemed larger, stronger on a face that had shrunken. Malid did not like the gray cast to Nimr's olive skin—only his black eyes were still sharp and alert. He looked thinner, too. Unhealthy, Malid would almost say. He wore only an open-necked shirt, charcoal-gray trousers and black leather loafers.

Malid faced him—but as always his father's presence left him feeling a boy of eight, a boy who could barely survive the desert. "I want to see my mother and then I will leave."

Nimr lifted one eyebrow. "You have not completed the deal. But I have come to a decision—ask for an additional fifteen percent of the income from the oil transported across my land."

Sucking in a breath, Malid stared at his father, his hands limp and shock cold on his skin. "Gordon Michaels will never agree to those terms."

"But he doesn't have to agree, does he? You only need to get his daughter to give you what you want."

Face hot, Malid took a step forward. "What do you imply? That Nigella is no better than a whore I can use? You know nothing of her, and it is beyond rude for you to insult her."

Both dark eyebrows rose. Nimr looked his son up and down, the look in his eyes calculating. "You have learned nothing yet. You may leave. If you do not, I will have the palace guard arrest you, and the police may bring charges. Was that not how you handled your brother's intended?"

Mouth tight, Malid turned on his heel. He stopped at the door and glanced back at his father. "This isn't over. I will see my mother, old man. And remember that when you are in your grave, I will be the son who inherits from you— that, you cannot change."

He slammed from the house and into the SUV. Fadin gave him a sideways glance, but Malid only said, "Drive."

With a nod, Fadin started the engine and pulled out of the courtyard. "Where to? Home?"

Malid muttered, "I have no home."

Fadin glanced at him. "Nimr has not changed. But if something does not change—if you cannot set aside your differences—another banishment or worse would be the only outcome. I am in no hurry to see you face such a thing again. Better perhaps to just live your life on your own terms?"

Looking at Fadin, Malid shook his head and asked, "Better for whom, Fadin? This is better for no one—not for me, for I gave Nigella my word on this deal. And now my father makes me a fool. What game is he playing at?"

\*\*\*

Nigella stood in the gardens of the Adjalane palace. The morning air was already heating up, but the lush gardens with their fountains and shaded overhangs provided nothing but cool places to sit and flowers that offered a riot of color. She turned and stared up at the building.

A dome rose from the center of the structure, with several small domes to the sides. The white stone walls gleamed in the sunlight, stark against the blue sky. She glanced at the wrought iron table and chairs with cushions and the mint tea left in a silver and gold service with small glasses trimmed in gold. A lovely spot—but why did Sheikh Nimr Adjalane want to see her? Why now? And why wasn't Malid here?

Nimr came out of the house. She'd seen photos of him, but she was surprised that he looked older in person— more gray in his black hair and beard, more lines around his mouth and face. He wore an Armani suit with a traditional white robe over it—meaning, this must be a formal meeting.

He waved at a chair and she sat. She had the feeling he needed to sit down and he wouldn't if she stayed standing.

After taking a seat and arranging his robes, he studied her a moment, poured tea, and then asked, "Did you hear that Malid came to the palace last night? We had…words."

Frowning, she shook her head. "I...I've been busy drawing up the papers for our deal."

A small smile curved his mouth. "Ah, the plans we make, and how so often they fail. I suspect my eldest son hates me at the moment, but the time to smooth that over is not something I have at my disposal. I need results and I need them yesterday."

She wiggled in her chair, trying to find a more comfortable spot. She'd worn a suit with pants and a silk shirt. It was already starting to feel too hot and confining. "I'm not sure I understand you," she said.

He sipped the tea and waved at the silver pot and tray. "Are you certain you won't take tea? This is a lovely hibiscus tea. No? Well, then let us get to matters. My sources say that you and Malid have become...close of late."

She stiffened. "How is that any of your business?"

Nimr waved a hand. "He is my son—my heir. Everything to do with him is something that affects the family. Let us be frank with one another." He leaned back. "I need my son where he should be—within the family. I wish him to do what he was raised to do, and I need to be confident that after I am gone, he will do things as I would. His arrogance caused him to betray his brother and almost ruined the relationship between Adilan and Michelle. A fine young woman, even though she is American."

Nigella bit her lower lip and shook her head. "You thought banishing him would provide what—a wake-up call?"

"Unfortunately, I did not factor in the extent of Malid's stubborn arrogance."

She gave him a tight smile. "I've heard him say that is a trait he shares with you."

Nimr's lips curved. "As you say—but without being tempered, it can prove a most dangerous trait." Head tipped to one side, he studied her. Nigella resisted the urge to fidget. He put down his tea and cleared his throat. "Do you care for my son?"

"As I said, I don't believe that is any of your business."

"Very well, let us talk business. I am willing to accept the deal that is—as you Americans might say—on the table. With one condition. You must help convince Malid to come home. Which would mean he must apologize for his past behavior."

Nigella suddenly wished she'd had taken that offer of tea—her mouth dried. She folded her hands in front of her and her pulse quickened. Nimr sounded as if he was ready to kill the deal if she didn't agree to this new term. "You think I have influence over Malid? That we have what…a relationship? We only met a few days ago."

Shoulders sagging, Nimr looked at her. He took a breath and seemed to shrink in on himself. "I am an old man. I need to know my son is back where he belongs, and that he has become a man others may trust and respect. I think…I see something in you that I believe Malid must see as well."

Nigella watched him carefully—what she saw was grief in his eyes, regrets. She gave a nod and chose her next words carefully. "You care about your son?"

Picking up his tea, Nimr said, "Bring Malid home—make him see sense. I get what I want, and you will get what you need—a deal that brings you your father's approval."

Sucking in a breath, Nigella held still. Nimr knew more than he was willing to say if he had guessed her reasons for being here.

He offered another, small smile, this one touched with something other than humor. "I have been waiting for Malid to come to me—to offer his sorrow for what was done. But he is still the man who must have things his way. I am aware your father is making noises of retiring—which means, this deal is your best chance to prove yourself to him in our world."

"Our world? What is that supposed to mean?" Nigella asked, wary again. Nimr was now reminding her far too much of Daddy—he was a damn cagey man.

Nimr waved a vague gesture. "The oil industry. A world created for and by men. A world where women are not readily accepted or trusted."

She shook her head. "I don't know if I have enough sway with Malid to convince him of much—he's very much his own man. You made him that, you know."

He nodded. "But I have found that when the heart is involved, any man can act for the good and approval of another. And, as you Americans like to say, what have you got to lose?"

She wet her lips. One word echoed in her head in answer—*everything.* She could end up losing the deal, and Malid's respect, and…and she didn't want to dig any deeper into that thought. What she'd had with Malid was…was what? A fling? She didn't do flings or affairs, and the thought right now of never seeing Malid again—or worse, seeing him and pissing him off by trying to interfere in his life—left her chest tight and her stomach knotted and she didn't want to go there. But what other choice did she have?

# Chapter 10

Nigella arrived back at her hotel, her mind spinning. If she didn't find a way to help Malid sort things out with his father, Nimr was never going to approve any deal with Opell Oil. Sure, she could fly to Tawzar—and end up with a terrible deal there.

She paced her hotel room, weighting her options. She could pretend the meeting with Nimr had never happened—and she'd lose everything. She could sweeten the deal—and Nimr would reject it. Or she could try and convince Malid to make peace with his father. Nimr was far too much like her own dad, and so she could speak from experience about dealing with a difficult father.

She stopped pacing and scowled at her pale reflection in the glass door that opened onto her balcony. "Even I can't pull that one off," she muttered.

Her cell phone rang, her dad's number showing up on the caller ID, so she answered.

"Nigella. How are things going? I haven't heard from you for a few days."

*Not an unusual occurrence, Daddy.* She buried her sarcasm—one family feud was enough right now—took a breath and put on her business voice. "Things are progressing." Boy—was that waffling.

Her father's Texas drawl deepened. "By that, I take it we're no closer to havin' a contract in hand."

"Actually, we are closer—there's a deal in place to buy the land. It's everything we need."

"But?" her father asked. That one word came loaded with doubt. "Tell you what, honey. I fly down an' we'll go see the sheikh together and button things up."

"Daddy, you said you were leavin' this to me." Nigella heard the drawl deepening in her voice, too.

"An' I have an' you got a deal done. But I want to start construction before summer kicks in and it's hotter than West Texas in a July. 'Sides, be nice to see my little girl."

Nigella clenched her back teeth. Once Daddy starting calling her 'his little girl' that meat he had stopped thinking of her as a woman who could run his company

*I have to fix this.*

Forcing a smile into her voice, she reminded Daddy he had a board meeting in London tomorrow—that would buy her a day. She hung up and dialed Malid's number. "It's Nigella Michaels."

She heard a smile in Malid's voice. "Did you think I wouldn't recognize you? I was just thinking of you. How are you?"

She paused, wishing she could take him up on the invitation she could hear lurking. But she was running out of time and options. "Can I come see you? Now?"

"What if I come to you? The helicopter will put me at your hotel in half an hour."

Nigella let out a breath. There were things about Malid's take-charge arrogance that were rather comforting. "Sounds good. I really didn't want to make the drive to you." She told him she'd meet him in the lobby, then started plotting just what she was going to say once she saw him. And was this all about to blow up in her face?

\*\*\*

Malid had heard the tension in Nigella's voice, and he saw it in her shoulders and stiff stance when he met her in the lobby. She looked in business mode—a dark suit coat and trousers, an even darker blouse. Her eyes seemed wary and she looked tired. Walking up to her, he took her hand. "Shall we get out of here?"

She gave a small smile. "Should I change first?" She waved her free hand at his jeans and polo shirt.

Malid grinned. "Today, I'm not a sheikh. And you'll be fine." He led her outside, flagged down a taxi and asked the driver to take them to the botanical gardens."

With a sideways glance, she said, "I didn't realize there was such a thing here."

"It is financed by both the Adjalane and the Sharqi families and has been likened to the Garden of Eden." He let his smile widen. "But it is not as private as an oasis."

Her cheeks warmed. He was delighted to see it. He had been hoping she might provide him the distraction he needed to forget his frustration and anger with his father. At least for a short while. But seeing her tense and worried, he found himself wanting to be the distraction for her. That was a novel sensation.

Twenty minutes later, he had her hand in his as they strolled along the paved walks amid the gardens that were shaded by trees and cooled by salt-tanged air from the ocean. Malid had bought them both iced lemonades.

Nigella had shed her suit coat and carried it over one arm. She looked far more relaxed now, but the worry had not left her eyes. "Hard to believe that not too far from here lies an inhospitable desert."

Malid shrugged. "What you deem inhospitable is home to many. Now, come sit and tell me what you wish to speak about?" He led her to a stone bench next to an arbor of jasmine.

Sitting down, Nigella draped her suit jacket next to her and turned to face him, her paper cup of lemonade crumpling in her hand. Malid took the cup from her and set it beside him, and she blurted out, "Your father asked to see me." Her mouth twisted. "He and my father have much in common."

He glanced at her. "You met with him." He made it a statement of fact and not a question. His stomach burned, but he swallowed back the reaction. He would wait and hear what had happened—but if Nimr had done anything to harm Nigella…

The urge to protect her surprised him—both for its heat and possessiveness. He had known her for so short a time. And yet in some ways it seemed as if she had been next to him forever. He didn't understand it, so he shook his head and frowned. "That cannot be a good thing."

She started to pleat a fold of her trousers. Malid put his hand over hers. "What troubles you?"

"My father's flying in. And yours…well, he's—"

"Impossible to deal with?"

She nodded. "But…well, have you ever wondered why he is?"

"Oh, I know. My father is the opposite of my grandfather—who nearly lost the family everything."

She wet her lips, and Malid wanted to lean in and kiss her. But she put a hand over his and said, "You mean he's afraid of the doing the same thing? Afraid even to show what he feels?"

"Are you speaking from your own experience?" Malid asked.

"No. I know my daddy loves me, he just doesn't think I have what it takes to run his company. He's trying to hang onto 'his little girl' being little."

Malid shook his head. "You're not trying to convince me that my father actually cares for me?" Pulling his hand from hers, he touched her cheek. "Do not even attempt to figure out the relationship between my father and me. I have been trying to do that for years with no success."

"Maybe that's 'cause you and your father are too much alike. You ever think what it'd be like to have a son like you? Someone always pushing, always thinking he knows better?"

Malid laughed. "A son…what ideas do you have in mind now?"

She pulled in a breath, and Malid said, "Why do I feel like I've just walked into a trap?"

Smiling, she leaned closer, to kiss the corner of his mouth, and trail kisses to his ear. "Will you do one thing for me?" she asked, her mouth pressed against his skin and her breath hot.

Malid closed his eyes. How could he deny her anything? Putting an arm around her waist, he pulled her closer. "You are playing unfair."

"What's that about love and war? And this is business. I have an idea."

"I have one as well," he said, pulling her even closer so her breasts pressed against his chest. He began to wish he had never thought of taking her away from her hotel—had met with her in her room so they could be having this conversation naked.

She pushed both hands against his chest and held him back. "First things first, and the first thing is—you've got a couple of brothers right?"

# Chapter 11

It took an hour to convince Malid to call his brother Nassir—the one he supposedly wasn't on the outs with.

They met him in an upscale restaurant that offered sheltered dining alcoves, and traditional low tables with cushioned seats that Nigella learned were called poufs. After they washed hands, the waiters brought the meal out—spicy chicken and grilled vegetables, something called a *mezze*, a plate with a lot of smaller dishes, including cheese, cubed melon, *tabbouleh*, *mutabbal*, and a grilled sausage, hummus, flatbread, and other side dishes that Nigella couldn't name. Back home, this would have been called a pot luck—but the dishes were far finer and rich. Nigella dug in and listened to the brothers talk.

It seemed that Nassir ran his own company and owned a gym. Like his father and Malid, he had dark hair and olive skin, a strong nose and lean features. But his eyes were a tawny brown, and the lines around his mouth came from an easy smile. Nigella found herself thinking, *Why couldn't I have fallen in love with this Adjalane?*

The thought froze her, and she started to choke on an olive. Malid patted her back, she grabbed for water and then stared at Malid.

*Love.* She was in love—falling, had fallen, was going deeper yet.

No—it couldn't be.

She stared at Malid, seeing the curve of his ear, how his beard always seemed to come into fast. She was short of breath and her head was buzzing. This couldn't be. She was a sensible person—she took her time with decisions. And yet…this wasn't just about business anymore. This wasn't about the deal. She wanted to see Malid happy— and that meant he needed to patch things up with his father. For his own sake. She wanted him happy because…because she'd done the thing she'd never done. She'd jumped in with both feet with him and she was in love with him.

Great—as if he'd want her to hang around once they got a deal done. She tore off some flatbread and chewed on it, not tasting a thing.

Nassir was telling his brother stories about his gym, and the bothers swapped some gossip. Nigella was glad to see there was at least one easy-going Adjalane around—maybe there was hope for this family after all.

After the meal had been cleared and a dessert of ice cream that tasted like roses was brought out—Nigella figured that had to be an acquired taste—she leaned forward and asked Nassir, "How is your mother?"

He stared at her. Malid cursed and said, "Father hasn't told you, has he?" Frowning, Nassir shook his head, and Malid said, "Mother is ill."

Face pale, Nassir shook his head again. "No. It can't be."

"Why not?" Malid asked. "You know Father. He tells us what he thinks we need to know—nothing more. When were you last at the palace?"

Nassir shifted his stare away. "I've been busy."

Nigella cut in before an argument could start. "That doesn't matter. Malid wants to see her—you should, too. And your daddy's being a butt about this." Both men stared at her and her cheeks heated. "Sorry, but he is."

Malid grinned, took her hand and kissed her knuckles. "No, that is the right word." He glanced back at Nassir. "Well, shall we go see mother?"

Nassir agreed to drive, but he warned Malid, "If Father sees you, he's going to want an apology."

Waving off that idea, Malid ushered Nigella into Nassir's truck. He climbed in after her. It wasn't exactly a family reunion, but it was a step, Nigella thought. The front seat was big enough to hold three, and she didn't mind pressing up against Malid—he didn't seem to mind, either, although he did seem distracted.

Nassir drove like a demon, leaving Nigella clutching Malid's arm. Nassir's truck was waved through the gates at the palace without a second glance. He'd barely stopped in the courtyard before Malid was out of the car and through the front doors. Nigella followed, leaving Nassir to deal with his truck, any guards, and possibly Malid's father.

Following Malid's echoing footsteps, Nigella headed down a hall and up a set of stairs. The place was huge, even bigger than she'd thought this morning—lord, was that only this morning she'd been here?

Malid threw open a set of double doors and stepped inside, and Nigella peaked in.

An older woman sat in a chair near tall windows that overlooked the garden. She looked comfortably plump, her dark hair long and worn up, her smile very much the same as Nassir's—welcoming and kind. To Nigella, Malid's mother looked healthy and alert. A mix of jasmine and roses scented the air. Glancing up, the woman smiled. "Malid. What a pleasant surprise." The soft melodic tone of her voice seemed strong to Nigella. If this woman was ill, it wasn't with anything serious.

Malid stopped as if he'd been hit by a two-by-four. His mouth fell open, worked a moment, and snapped closed. He stiffened, his hands fisting at his sides. "Mother, you're not...I was told you were ill?"

She smiled and reached for Malid's hand. "Does your father know you are here? Have you made it up with him? Who is this lovely young lady you have brought to see me?"

Malid spat out his next words. "Father hinted to me that you were dying."

She let out a sigh. "Ah, Nimr—always trying to manage everyone. It is not me who must see a doctor. It is Nimr. He is refusing to undergo the treatments that might prolong his life."

# Chapter 12

Malid's skin chilled and his heart seemed to stop. He stared at his mother, the blood pounding in his temples. "Nimr is dying?" The words stuck on his tongue. It seemed impossible.

His mother stood and patted him on the chest. "Please talk with him. You must make it right. It's not good for a family to be at war with one another—and it is not good for Nimr."

Malid forced a smile and took his mother's hand. "As long as you are well, that is all that matters." He turned and started for the door, and saw Nigella standing there, shifting from one foot to the other. He ought to introduce her. Instead, he waved from Nigella to his mother. "Mother, this is Nigella. Please see she is made welcome." With that, he left.

He headed for where he thought Nimr must be—in his study. The spider sitting at the heart of his web. It was time they had done with all deceptions.

His father's study was a room he had come to hate—comfortable leather chairs, books lining one wall, paintings on two of the other walls, French doors that opened into the garden. Malid could only remember the times he had been left standing here, facing his father's desk, waiting for his father's disapproval.

Stepping into the room, Malid saw his father look up. Nimr put down a pen he had been writing with and folded his hands, his dark eyebrows lifted. "You have thought better of your words?"

"We had an arrangement."

Nimr frowned. "I see you still have not thought about anything."

Malid threw out a hand. "The mighty Nimr Adjalane—don't you ever tire of acting the puppet master who makes us all dance?"

Standing, Nimr put his hands flat on his desk. "How dare you speak to me like that!"

"And how dare you use my mother as a pawn. She isn't ill. You are—but I would call it a sickness in the head." Malid jabbed a finger at his father.

Nimr straightened and slashed a hand though the air. "None of that matters. And our arrangement was for you to negotiate with Opell Oil—once you had a deal, I would give permission for you to visit. I was hoping you would learn more than you have."

Malid took a step forward. "I worked out an excellent deal. I don't know what devil drives you, but I will not play your games, and I no longer must live by your rules."

"From what I can see, you don't live by any rules. Everything I have tried to do has been for your own good—but you are too blind to see. You are an Adjalane and you belong here to take the family forward. But no…you cannot see that. How did you even get in here?"

"Nassir brought me."

Nimr frowned and sat down suddenly. He clutched his left arm with his right hand. His skin took on an odd pallor—and fatigue filled his eyes. Malid held still, suspecting yet another ploy—another trick. Nimr was never sick—never. He thought of what Nigella had said— that Nimr could not express what he felt. And his mother had said his father was the one who was ill. Well, it did not matter—nothing did. Malid turned to go—he would not be back.

Before he could, Hassan—Nimr's servant—came into the room and said, "Gordon Michaels is here to see you."

# Chapter 13

Malid watched as his father tried to pull the cloak of his position around him. He straightened and let go of his arm—but Malid felt as if he'd just seen the first chink in his father's armor. It made him seem human, something Malid would have sworn would never happen.

Ignoring Malid, Nimr glanced at Hassan. "Show him in."

Gordon Michaels came in as if he had been lurking right behind Hassan. The man looked rushed, his face slightly reddened, his hair tousled. His suit seemed wrinkled by travel and his tie looked as if it had hurriedly been pushed into place. However, Malid knew this was a man to reckon with. From all he had heard, Gordon Michaels had perfected the look of a country-boy—but his reputation was of a shark. Nigella trailed into the room behind him, and sent a frown and a small shake of her head at Malid, as if she had spoken already to her father to try and avert this and had failed.

Malid narrowed his eyes—he would not sit back and watch Gordon Michaels treat Nigella poorly.

Pushing his hands into his pockets, he watched as Gordon Michaels stalked into the room. "Adjalane, just what game you playin' at? Are we doing a deal or runnin' in circles?"

Nimr shrugged. "No game. You want something that is very important to myself and my family. I want something in return."

Arms crossed, Gordon waited. Malid stepped forward to say something, but Nigella walked between the two older men. "Well, isn't this just fine. You two can now have a good row that won't make anyone feel better." She glanced at Malid. "Malid, you have a chance to mend things here."

He stiffened. "Nigella, why do you ask that of me?"

She threw out her arms. "For one thing, I'd like y'all to stop using anger and bluster as a reason not to say what you're feeling. Family is important—to all of us." She blew out a breath. "You and I, Malid, we have something going. But right now my heart is breaking 'cause I could never be with a man who would abandon his family."

Malid stepped back—he felt as if she had slapped him. "You expect me to forgive everything my father has done?"

"What about what you've done? Families fight, but at the end of the day, they stick together. Without family, we have nothing." She turned and stared at her father. "Daddy, I love you, but I'm done with trying to prove myself to you." She turned to Malid's father. "Sir, you might have been trying to teach your son a lesson, but it's about as good as the one of you leavin' him in the desert—just plain wrong-headed." Finally, she looked at Malid. "And you...you make a fine third here, just as bull-headed as these two and trying to get your own way and ready to stomp off if you don't."

Malid stared at her for a moment, his heart pounding. He glanced at his father and Nigella's father—the two men looked stunned. Nimr sat back in his chair, one hand pressed to his chest. Gordon lifted a hand and let it drop. "Honey, you're my little girl."

"Not any more, Daddy. I'm grown, and if you don't put me in charge, I'll find a company that will. Won't mean I love you any less, and I know you love me." She propped a hand on her hip and faced Malid. "As for you—well, you need to make a choice here between pride or losing everything worth having. And that might include me since I'm not so sure I can be with a guy who doesn't know how to say those three very important words?"

"Words? What...I love you?"

"Those are nice, but I'm thinking more of saying, I'm sorry."

Malid stared at her—how dare she...she...she tell him the truth. He blinked. For the first time in his life, he knew he wanted something more than just to be in the right. The thought of not having Nigella in his life twisted a knot in his guts--.

He took a step toward her and stopped.

What if he said those words she had asked for—offered up an apology—but his father threw them away? Would Nigella blame him? His father was the hardest man in the world to deal with—and Malid wasn't certain he could back down here.

He looked from his father to Nigella's father and nodded. "It seems my father is not well. Until he is fully recovered, I will be acting for him—and we will sign our deal." Nimr made a sound of protest, but Malid stepped between him and Gordon. "Father, you wished an apology. You do not deserve it. But if what you want is for me to make amends to my brother and his new wife, that I can do. I will do what is necessary to convince you to let me finish these negotiations." Malid turned to Gordon. "But I will only sign this deal with Nigella Michaels."

Gordon looked between Malid and his father. "I guess we could do that."

Nimr started to stand. Before he could, he gave a gasp and fell back in his chair, clutching his chest. Malid moved at once to his father's side, felt for a pulse in his wrist and found it racing. Yelling for Hassan, he ordered the man to fetch Nassir at once.

Nigella came over and put a hand on Malid's shoulder. "What's wrong?"

Malid shook his head, and Nassir burst into the room. "I think he's having a heart attack. He needs to get to the hospital immediately."

Nassir bent down over his father. "Malid, there's a sandstorm brewing. It won't be safe."

Malid shook his head. "It will if I drive. Nigella, will you—?"

"I'm coming with," she said, her tone flat and final.

# Chapter 14

For a moment, Nigella thought Malid would argue with her. His mouth flattened, but the worry hadn't left his eyes. She knew the danger—sandstorm. The sand could clog the engine—they could be trapped. But Malid gave a nod. Nassir, do you have scarves in your truck? Nassir gave a nod.

Malid and Nassir got their arms around their father. He grumbled a protest, but nothing more, and they picked him up as if he weighted nothing. Nigella hurried to the front doors to throw them open for him.

Calling out, Malid shouted, "Mr. Michaels, after the storm passes, please escort my mother to the hospital, and have Hassan send someone to find our brother, Adilan. He should be there as well."

Outside, the wind had picked up. Nigella smelled the dry warmth of the desert and the bite of sand stung her cheeks. She could already see the sky darkening to brown in the west. "How long?" she asked Malid. She yanked open the doors to the truck—it was an extended cab. Malid and Nassir settled Nimr in the back seat, Nigella climbed in with him and fastened his seatbelt and hers. She took Nimr's hand in hers—his pulse seemed erratic, but he was still aware and grumbling, telling everyone there was no need for such fuss.

Nigella fixed a stare on him. "Do you really want to die and leave Malid in charge?"

He frowned at her and said, his voice gravely, "You are impertinent."

"So I've been told." She dug into her purse and pulled out a small bottle of aspirin." Opening it, she dug one out. "Chew and swallow. It'll taste horrible, but it's the best think for heart attack and that's my guess for what you're having. If it's not, it's not a stroke and the aspirin won't hurt." Nimr stared at her. She raised her eyebrows. "It's your choice about the dying part—but I think your boys are trying to keep you around."

Still grumbling about Western women who didn't know their place, Nimr took the aspirin and chewed. Nigella glanced out the window. The sand made spitting noises as it hit the vehicle, and the sky had darkened even more, leaving the sun a red ball in the dirty sky. She found the headscarves Nassir had said he had in his car—tucked into a plastic bag. She dug one out for herself, then one for Nimr. He grumbled even more and pulled it from her hands, but his fingers trembled. She took it from him and began to put it in place as best she could.

Malid and Nassir had had a brief argument over who would drive, but Malid had won simply by climbing into the driver's seat and buckling in. Nassir was forced to jump into the passenger's side before Malid took off with a squeal of tires.

Gulping down a breath, Nigella figured this would be a wild ride, but Malid navigated his way with almost an instinct for how to stay on the road. She didn't bother him with questions, but when it became almost impossible to see more than a few feet in front of the car, she turned her attention back to Nimr. He, too, kept his eyes closed. His breathing was fast and shallow. Sweat stood out on his forehead.

Nigella felt a stare on her. She wet her lips and looked up and met Malid's stare in the rear view mirror—for once he wasn't the cocky, arrogant man. He looked a worried son. And then he had to look back at the road.

The truck jerked to a stop. Nigella braced herself and started to ask what had happened. But Nassir and Malid jumped from the truck and came around to get their father out—they had to be at the hospital.

Above the howl of the wind, Malid yelled to Nigella, "Go inside. Tell them what's happened."

Nigella fumbled with her seatbelt, got it off, struggled with the door, and stepped out—the wind almost slammed her back. She grabbed her flapping scarf and got one end over her mouth. Hunched over, she ran for the brightest light, hoping that was the emergency room light from glass doors. It was. The double doors opened for her and closed, and then an interior set opened. She stepped back into a calm world, and got out the words, "Heart attack. Sheikh Adjalane."

The staff jumped as if she'd hit them with a cattle prod. A gurney appeared, nurses rushed for the doors. Malid came in with Nassir, their father held between them, Malid coughing form the sand dust, and Nassir's face hidden by his headscarf.

A flurry of activity erupted. Nimr was settled on the gurney, IV bags appeared along with monitors and cuffs and other equipment, and just as fast Nimr was whisked away.

Rubbing her arms, Nigella stepped up to Malid. "You okay?"

He shook his head. "I do not matter—but my father is in good hands. He built this hospital, so they will be aware of that. Knowing that their major benefactor is now a patient is a motivating force."

Nigella managed a weak smile. Nassir headed over to the desk, Malid followed and the two began to answer questions put to them—when had the pain started, had he ever had anything like this before. Nigella interrupted to explain she had given Sheikh Adjalane an aspirin. The nurse nodded and kept asking questions—and then they were told to wait.

Sheikh Adjalane had been taken to the lab for cat scans and testing. Nassir yanked off his head scarf and strode away, calling back, "I am going for some tea."

Malid turned to Nigella—and she saw in his eyes the fear that she would feel if it was her father in a hospital like this. Walking to him, she put her arms around him and held him tight. Malid stiffened a moment, then leaned into her, wrapping his arms around her.

*** 

Malid paced the waiting room. Nigella had gone to wash her face and use the facilities. Nassir was off, asking the nurses yet again about their father. Malid knew there was nothing to do but wait—he hated that. He wanted to do something—but this was up to the doctors.

He had thought about calling in specialists—but they were already here. All he could do now was ask for a private room and round-the-clock nursing once his father was out of heart surgery. They had been informed that the tests had shown a blockage—it was being corrected with stents that would open up the arteries again.

Hearing a door open, Malid turned, expecting Nassir—or a nurse. Instead, Adilan took a step in and paused.

He hadn't seen his brother in months—and he hadn't been to his brother's wedding. He regretted that now, and glanced behind Adilan, looking for the American woman, Michelle, that Adilan had married.

Adilan lifted one dark eyebrow. "Michelle is parking the car."

Malid shrugged. "Ever the independent woman." Adilan stiffened, and Malid came forward. Guilt tugged at him, a small twist in his chest.

Stepping into the room, Adilan asked, "How is he?"

Malid lifted a hand. "I think it will take more than one small attack to kill our father."

"Were you arguing?"

Malid looked at his brother. "No, I was trying to give him an apology—but I believe it really should go to you. Or your wife. I was wrong."

Adilan rubbed his jaw. He had filled out even more in the past few months—even though he was the youngest, he had always had more muscle. Now he looked—a man, not a boy. Married life agreed with him. Frowning, he stepped forward. At last he extended his hand. "Brother should argue, but we should also know when to stop. Father has been tired of late. Mother keeps asking him to have tests done, but you know Father."

"He didn't want to hear that he should slow down. Did you know he called me to negotiate a deal with Opell Oil?"

Adilan huffed out a laugh. "Ah, that is why I saw Gordon Michaels at the palace. I thought perhaps he'd been there to see father."

"He was."

Shaking his head, Adilan sat down in one of the chairs. The waiting room was a private one, but it still had the world's most uncomfortable chairs, Malid thought. Hard backs and seats designed to keep you awake and on your feet. Adilan asked, "How long have you been here?"

Malid shook his head. "I don't really know. It seems forever."

Adilan nodded. "Mother will be here as soon as the storm passes."

"So you drove in it, too?" Malid asked.

Before Adilan could answer, the door opened and an older man in blue hospital scrubs stepped in. His name badge read Dr. Azoula, and he shook hands with Malid and then with Adilan, and asked if their brother needed to be here.

"You are caring for my father? How is he?" Adilan asked.

Malid waved for the doctor to talk. The man nodded and said, "It was good you got him to the hospital as fast as you did. A blockage such as the one he had can damage the heart—time is vital to restore circulation. The procedure went very well, but he will need rest for a complete recovery."

"Can we see him?" Adilan asked.

"Soon as we have him settled. And don't expect him to wake for a few hours." The doctor left and Adilan glanced at Malid. "It seems I owe you a debt, brother."

Nassir stepped into the room, steaming tea in his hand. "A debt for what?" he asked.

Turning, Adilan grinned. "It's right that Malid is back home. And if Father has a problem with it, I will go with you to talk to him."

"You will?" Nassir shook his head. "We will. But I think…why don't we let that conversation wait for a time."

"Is Michelle on her way here?" Nassir asked. Adilan nodded. Nassir glanced from Malid to Adilan. "And she's going to be okay seeing him? She doesn't have a knife on her, does she?"

Adilan grinned. "If she does, Malid will have to look out for himself."

Shaking his head, Malid pulled open the door. "Go, you to. Make sure Father is comfortable. I'll bring Michelle up when she arrives."

Nassir shook his head. "You always had more courage than sense."

Malid smiled. "No. I have a secret weapon." Adilan frowned, Nassir grinned, and the two men strode out, heading for the elevators. They passed Nigella on the way, and Malid saw Nassir give her a wink.

She came over to Malid's side. "That's got to be another Adjalane—your father must have made the three of you out of the same mold."

"I think my mother had something to do with it." He wrapped an arm around her waist, and told her the doctor's news.

She let out a breath and smiled. "I'll bet your mother's going to love having to keep your daddy resting."

"No, that will be the job of the staff, and Hassan has been managing my father for decades. Hassan will find ways to ensure my father's rest, without seeming to do anything. There will simply be a lack of phone calls, few visitors will stay to tire my father, and papers will not be on my father's desk when he demands them."

Her eyes widened. "I need to get my daddy a Hassan. Can we go see Nimr? Should I wait here?"

He took her hand and stepped from the room, and saw Michelle walking into the hospital. She looked much as he remembered—a very straight nose, wide-spaced blue eyes, and the olive complexion of a woman from his own country. Her almost black hair was worn straight, and she had on a light-colored business suit, with a short hem. Malid was quite certain Michelle would never adapt fully to the customs of his country. Disapproval for her dress rose in him, but he bit it back.

Michelle saw him, glanced away and back. She missed one step and the color drained from her face.

Frowning, Malid pulled Nigella with him and headed for Michelle—Nigella would have to help him make this right. But Nigella pulled from her hand away from his and stepped forward, one hand offered. "You must be Michelle. Adilan is upstairs. I'm Nigella Michaels. I have to say I saw your wedding photos in the newspapers when I was doing my homework for the deal I was putting together for Opell Oil and the Adjalanes, but the photos don't do you justice."

Michelle blinked, and Malid had to hide a smile—he had never seen her at a loss for words like this. "Why…thank you." She sounded uncertain and she turned to Malid, her eyes sparking with a challenge and her back stiff. "I'm surprised your back. Come to make trouble?"

Malid smiled. "I've already apologized to Adilan, and I offer you my regrets as well. I—" He glanced at Nigella, saw she'd lifted her eyebrows as if she knew what he should say and was waiting. Ah, but this woman would tie him in knots. He grinned. He would not mind so long as he, too, was allowed to play with knots when they were alone. He turned back to Michelle. "I will understand if you are unable to forgive me."

She tipped her head to one side, her eyes narrowed, and then Michelle lifted a fist and punched his arm. It hurt—it actually hurt. Rubbing the spot, he stared at her. She grinned. "I've been wanting to do that for far too long. And Adilan's been giving me boxing lessons. You can be the worst jerk…but Adilan…I think he's missed you, you bastard."

Malid heard a choked laugh. He glanced at Nigella, saw her covering her mouth. He looked at Michelle and gave a small bow. "Do we call it even now?"

Michelle shook her head. "Brother, I'm just getting started. But I suppose a hospital is a place for a truce."

With a wave, he allowed her to head into the elevator first—he didn't want that woman at his back.

Nimr had been settled into a private room, but the staff wanted only one visitor at a time. Malid found himself in a private waiting room, not far from his father. Nigella stood close to him, and he realized He couldn't have done this without her. But how could he tell her that—they had known each other such a short time.

His mother came out of Nimr's room looking tired and drawn. Adilan swapped a look with his wife, and Michelle offered to take their mother to get some tea. That was a good idea. Nigella leaned close to Malid and said, "He's your father. You can't fool me, you know. You care about him but you just don't know how to show it."

Malid slanted a look at her. "How do you know that?"

"You want me to list the reasons? There's the fact that you didn't leave the region after he banished you."

"Al-Sarid is my home. I always planned on finding a way back."

"And you broke your own rule—you went out in a sandstorm in order to get your father the help he needed."

He shook his head. "Anyone would have done the same."

Nigella smiled. "Really? But then we come to your hand."

"What does my hand have to do with it?" he asked.

She smiled and put a hand on his arm. "I've seen the tremors in your fingers—you were worried for him. Afraid he would die. I've been through this with Daddy—he had a stroke scare that had me climbing the walls." She nodded to Nimr's room. "Go on. I'll wait here with your brothers."

He squeezed her hand and headed into his father's room.

Nimr lay on his bed, his eyes closed, wires hooked up to monitors and a tube to give him oxygen attached to his nose. Shifting on his feet, Malid wondered what he should do—what should he say. He had no idea, so he simply thought of Nigella and how she had stayed close to him, even holding his hand. He had never seen the man look so…so quiet.

Malid sat down next to the bed on a hard chair and clasped his father's hand between his own.

Nimr's eyes fluttered and opened slightly. He parted his lips and his voice came out raspy and weak. "Never go out in a sandstorm. Did I not teach you better?"

Malid shook his head. "I was confident I could get us to the hospital. Hassan taught me to drive. You had me worried today—but…but it made me realized something very important. Family must come first—before business. Before anything."

Nimr gave a snort and then coughed. Malid stood and picked up the water on the table next to Nimr's bed. He helped his father take two sips. Nimr held up a hand, and Malid put down the water and sat again.

"You will be glad, Father, to know I have made things right between myself and Adilan—and Michelle as well."

Lifting one dark eyebrow, Nimr stared at him. "Have you?" He narrowed his eyes. "You have been different today—is this the work of that American girl?"

"What if it is?"

Nimr let out a sigh. "My sons seems doomed to fall in love with Americans."

Smiling, Malid shook his head. "Did you not fall in love with an American woman—before she left you and broke your heart, and you had to marry mother instead."

Nimr groaned. "My chest hurts. I think I will sleep."

"Oh, no—you do not get away from me so easily."

Nimr waved a hand. "See Hassan. I have already set up the documents you need to act in my place." Malid stared at his father. A small smile curved Nimr's mouth. "What— you think I did not know you would come around…eventually. You were right to intervene with Gordon Michaels, and you have my permission to make whatever deal you think is right. And, if you let that pretty American slip through your fingers, you are not as smart as I think you are. Now go away. Let Nassir come in—he is as peaceful as your mother. I will see Adilan after, and then I plan to sleep."

Malid stood. "Yes, Father."

Nimr chuckled. "Ah, if only you were such a dutiful son."

"That would mean I am not your son." Malid squeezed his father's hand and put it back down on the white sheets. He headed out, a weight seeming to lift from his shoulders.

He told Nassir to go in next, and then he turned to Nigella. "Come. You look as tired as I feel."

"What a charming thing to say to a lovely woman," Adilan said. He glanced at Nigella. "IS he always so charming to you?"

She shook her head. "Only when he wants something."

Grabbing Nigella's hand, Malid pulled her with him to the elevators. "Please, let us go. I hate the smell of hospitals and—"

"And almost losing your father…it's hard."

He looked at her. He had almost lost his father today, and suddenly all of their fighting seemed insignificant. Getting his own way would mean nothing if he lost the people who meant the most to him in the process.

The elevator arrived. He stepped in and pulled Nigella close. "Will you come home with me?"

"Why don't we head to the nearest hotel—it's faster and you'll want to be close to your dad."

He laughed. "Beautiful as well as smart—I am a lucky man."

Smiling, she put her arms around his neck. "Oh, you're about to get very lucky."

# Chapter 15

Malid flagged down a taxi and directed it to the nearest hotel. Too much excitement had left Nigella both tired and at the same time she knew she wouldn't be able to sleep—she also wanted her skin pressed against Malid's. Tomorrow they could go back to hashing out business terms—tonight…tonight she just wanted to feel Malid's heart beating against hers.

The nearest hotel proved to be both luxurious and Nigella didn't want to even think about the cost. Malid checked them in with a flourish—it seemed there were many advantages to the Adjalane name. Room service brought them sparkling water, a meal of roast meats and salads, and a dessert of something with a light pastry, honey and dates.

Nigella didn't wait for the room service, but had headed straight for the shower, tearing off her clothes as she went. She came out with a towel wrapped around her to find that Malid had the lights low and the meal set out on the balcony.

She glanced at him and asked, "Can the food wait?" He nodded, his eyes darkening. She smiled. "Good," she said and dropped her towel.

In two strides Malid was at her side, swept her into his arms and carried her into the bedroom. He settled her on the bed, tore off his shirt and slipped his shoes and jeans off.

God, how she loved his body—every muscular line, every inch of smooth skin. She opened her arms and he came to her, covering her with his body, slipping into her at once.

She gave a sigh, wiggled her hips and he rolled with her, so that she straddled him. "Now—you may take your pleasure."

Smiling, she did. She eased her hips up…and down again, dragging a long, soft moan from him. His eyes slid closed, so she did it again. And again. But already the heat was building inside her. Tingles spread over her skin.

Opening his eyes, Malid reached between them and touched her clit—that touch shivered over her and sank deep. Closing her eyes, she threw her head back and let the world come apart.

*** 

They slept, ate, made love in the shower, and slept again. Nigella woke early, found Malid asleep next to her, his erection nudging her hip. She threw back the sheets, brushed her fingers over his cock, and leaned over to take him into her mouth. He moaned and came awake at once. It took a lot not to giggle at his gasp of pleasure, but she managed, sucking hard and licking until he grabbed her shoulders and pulled her down on the bed so he could enter her.

After, they showered and dressed—Malid made a face at his wrinkled clothes, so he made a call and fresh jeans and shirts appeared for both of them.

Staring at the clothing, Nigella asked, "Just how did you know my size."

He put his hands on her hips. "How could I not?"

They visited Sheikh Adjalane, only to find a line of well-wishers and a room full of flowers. The nursing staff looked flustered at trying to control the flow of visitors, and Malid took charge after one nurse muttered, "He should rest."

In less than five minutes, Malid had the visitors ushered out with smiles, the flowers sent to any new mother who had just given birth, and was lecturing his father on his care.

Nigella could see Nimr's mouth start to pull down, so she started to tug at Malid's arm. "Don't we have a contract to sign."

Malid agreed that was true, ordered his father to rest, and walked out—and Nigella could swear the old man looked relieved.

A week later, the deal was done—Nigella's was relieved both for that and the fact that Daddy had gone back to the States, and Nimr was allowed back home.

It was over—finished. She had no reason to stay…so why was she hanging around? It was time to give Malid a kiss, tell him it had been fun, and let him get back to his family. She had work waiting for her—so why wasn't she grabbing the next jet home?

***

It took Malid an hour to convince Nigella she must make one last visit to the desert. She had been making noises about going home—something must be done about that.

His father was home again, the deal with Opell Oil was set, and now he could focus on her. But did she want to stay? For once in his life, he was uncertain what a woman might say to him—and worried the answer might be no. It had never mattered before...but Nigella mattered. And his father's near brush with death had brought home just how short life could be.

He drove her back to the oasis—as he had once before. Nigella's face had lit with excitement, and that had pleased Malid. The tents were few this time—just one for Malid and Nigella. They would keep no servants with them.

Adilan was overseeing the construction of the pipeline—it was only right since he was CEO of Adjalane Oil. And Nassir was helping their mother look after their father.

And still Malid was worried. Would Nigella think this was nothing more than a plan to intertwine their families permanently? In an age-old tradition, such family ties had built empires. But that was not what he wanted.

Taking Nigella into the tent with him, he closed the cloth fastening over the door and secured it. Lamps lit the tent—pillows and tapestries made the space intimate and comfortable. A low, brass table had been set with food and water. Malid ignored all of that and pulled Nigella into his arms.

They had dressed in traditional robes—and he approved of that. Her breasts pressed into him—already he wanted her out of those clothes.

"Nigella—?"

"Is this our last night together?" She lifted her chin. She looked fragile in the lamplight—delicate, and not the strong woman he knew her to be.

He touched a finger to her face. "I wish it to be the first of many."

She frowned. "You want me to move to Al-Sarid?"

Rubbing his hands down her arm, he shook his head. "I was thinking more that we split our time. Adjalane Oil needs New York offices. And Adilan thinks I should be in charge of setting up that division. We need to look to the future—to expand and change from just oil to newer technologies."

Her eyebrows arched high. "Is this a business deal we're making?"

Cursing, he let go of her, turned and rubbed the back of his neck, then faced her, his hands spread wide. "I am doing this all wrong. It sounded so good in my head, and now…now it sounds like the howl of a desert wind."

"You've become very philosophical." Nigella stepped closer. "Why don't you try saying what you feel—instead of any kind of rehearsed speech." She put her hands on his chest.

He sucked in a breath. "I cannot think when you touch me."

Smiling, she nodded. "That's a good start."

Malid dipped his head, nuzzling her ear and whispering in her ear, "What I have to say is important."

Nigella hummed and said, "Yes, so is this. Am I a distraction?"

"Of the best kind." He pulled off her head scarf and tunic. She tugged off his shirt. "Nigella, I will want you forever." He slipped one hand beneath the waistband of her trousers. She kissed his mouth and trailed kisses over his jaw line.

Quickly, he stripped her of her remaining clothing. Laying down, she spread herself on the pile of pillows, her white skin almost seeming to shimmer in the light. He pulled off his trousers and lay down next to her. Gripping her hips, he pulled her up onto him.

"Ride me," he urged her, lifting her up slightly and then settling her over himself. He eased her down gently, and guided her movements until he couldn't resist palming her breasts one more second.

She threw back her head and smiled. Slowly, hips moving, she brought her gaze back to his. He pulled her down to capture her lips with his own. She moaned into his mouth, and shivered, and his own orgasm took him in gentle waves that seemed to last a life time.

Nigella collapsed against his chest, her breathing fast and her body limp. Sweat slicked her skin, and Malid rubbed a hand down her back. "Nigella, you once told me you do not make leaps—you want careful decisions. But I am going to ask you now to leap."

She turned to stare at him, her eyes wide and huge. He drew a finger down her cheek. "I love you. I want to spend the rest of my life with you. Will you marry me? Will you camp with me in the desert and help me weather sandstorms? Will you help me figure out better ways of getting along with people? Will you…will you be part of my family?"

Nigella wet her lips, and Malid held his breath. She lifted one pale shoulder and rolled off him so she lay next to him. She trailed a fingertip over his chest. "You know I like to consider all angles."

He frowned. "Yes. And what angles must you consider."

"Well, do you like and want children?"

"Do you?"

"No fair—I asked first."

He threw out a hand. "Yes, I want children."

"Good. So do I. Two. What about my working?"

Impatient, he caught her hand and rolled up onto one elbow. "What about it? You wish to stop?"

"No…not when Daddy's finally thinkin' I can run the company."

"Good. You have too much energy to waste it lounging around a palace."

She laughed. "Does that mean I get my own palace?"

Malid rolled her over so that he was above her. He dipped his head and kissed her, then shifted, reaching to the low brass table. He pulled a silk wrap off the table and put it into her hands. She tugged open the knot and a sapphire ring of dark blue fell into her fingers. She gasped, and Malid said, "Not only a palace, but all the riches I can shower on you."

He could see she was fighting a smile, but she shook her head, clutched the ring and asked, "You don't think our fathers ever suspected this might happen when they put us in charge of these negotiations, do you? So they could get some grandbabies?"

Malid looked at her and laughed. Taking the ring from her, he held it out. "Let us hope they are not such manipulators, but I don't care. If putting us together was their way of controlling us, I owe them gratitude."

Nigella pushed her finger into the ring. She tilted her hand to make the gem sparkle, then settled herself across his chest. "Maybe we should send them a thank you card?"

"How about a wedding announcement?" He kissed her forehead, then her lips, and murmured against her lips, "Always and forever, Nigella. You have my soul in your hands. *Enta habib alby w hayaty ya habibi.* You are the love of my heart and my life, my love."

Smiling, she slid her hand behind his neck. "Big words—how about you set about provin' it to me?"

Grinning, he rolled her underneath him—and took his time pleasing his bride to be.

# *END OF* The Sheikh's Reluctant American

Book Three of the Adjalane Sheikhs Series.

Want more Leslie North?

# Thank You!

Thank you so much for purchasing, downloading and reading my book. It's hard for me to put into words how much I appreciate my readers. If you enjoyed it, please remember to leave a review for it. I love hearing from my readers! I want to keep you guys happy :). For all books by Leslie North go to:

## Leslie North's Amazon Page

## OR Visit Her Website: LeslieNorthBooks.com

**Get FIVE full-length, highly-rated Leslie North Novellas FREE! Over 548 pages of best-selling romance with a combined 421 FIVE STAR REVIEWS!**

**Sign-up to her mailing list and start reading them within minutes:**

## www.LeslieNorthBooks.com/sign-up-for-free-books

# The Sharqi Sheikhs Series

## The Sheikh's Unforgettable Lover

The Sheik's Accidental Pregnancy

The Sheik's Defiant Girlfriend

The Sheikh's Demanding Fiancée

The Sheikha's Determined Police Officer

**The Jawhara Sheiks Series**

The Sheik's Pregnant Bride (FREE) – Excerpt Below!

The Sheik's Troublesome Bride

The Sheik's Captive Bride

**The Fedosov Family Series**

The Russian's Stubborn Lover (FREE)

The Russian's Bold American

The Russian's Secret Child

# The Sheikh's Unforgettable Lover (The Sharqi Sheikhs Series Book One)

Kim Atkins watched Sheik Karim Sharqi lift free weights on the courtyard below her, sweat glistening off his body in the intense sunlight. Staring down at him, she had never seen a man so strong, so muscular, so alluring, as she imagined that perfect body pressed against hers, his hands holding her waist as she stroked his rippling muscles.

Kim turned her head to see three maids watching him from a distance. One of them was fanning herself as they whispered and giggled amongst themselves. Kim did not blame them -- Karim Sharqi was a very attractive man.

Closing her eyes, she imagined herself looking into his eyes, his dark hair neatly framing his face as his brown eyes smiled down at her. In her mind, she fisted her hand to keep from touching his perfectly straight nose perched atop luscious lips that invited her to lean in for a kiss.

She briefly wondered what his stubble would feel like rubbing against her fevered skin, as he kissed his way down her body. She swayed slightly on her feet as her all too active imagination made her body tingle at the thought of his touch.

"Does this sentence make sense?" Amare asked, interrupting her daydream.

"Huh?" Kim snapped out of her thoughts and returned her attention to Amare. She had forgotten where she was and what she was doing. "Sorry, show me," she said and took the notebook from him.

Kim had originally come to Saudi Arabia as an ESL (English as Second Language) teacher and when her contract was over, she was fortunate enough to be hired as a private tutor for Amare, the youngest son of Sheik Saeed Sharqi.

"Well done," Kim said, as she handed the notebook back to him.

"Thanks."

"You're doing really well, Amare."

"Really? I am?"

Kim grinned at him, tousling his hair, "Yes, you are."

"Cool. Father expects me to excel on all my exams," he told her as he squeezed the notebook before setting it down.

"I have no doubt that you will." Kim smiled at the young sheik. She was impressed with how hard he was working. When she had first accepted the job, she did not expect to meet such a serious student. In her experience, children born with silver spoons in their mouths tended not to work very hard.

"Not only should I work hard, I should be top of my class," Amare said solemnly.

Kim raised her eyebrows. "That is a lot of pressure."

"My father wants nothing but the best."

Kim sighed. She had heard that the Sheik was strict but she could not believe how much pressure he was putting on his son. She was glad that she had not been raised with that much expectation to do well in school. She flipped open her folder and pulled out a poem.

"We'll do the best we can," she said, handing him a sheet of paper. "See if you can interpret this poem for me."

"Sure."

Whilst Amare was reading the poem, Kim's gaze travelled back to the courtyard below. Karim was still outside in the courtyard working out and was currently doing push-ups on the slate tiled floor. The muscles in his back tensed up as he bent his arms and slowly lowered himself down.

He had taken off his shirt and his torso was bathed in sweat as Kim contemplated licking the salty sweat from his chest. Lost in thought, she watched as he reached for a towel and slowly dried the sweat from his body leaving Kim to wonder what it would feel like to stroke her fingers along those rock hard abs.

A noise from behind her made her jump as she finally realised that Karim was looking straight at her with a smirk on his face. She gasped and looked away quickly.

"Crap," she muttered under her breath.

<u>**The Sheikh's Unforgettable Lover (The Sharqi Sheikhs Series Book One)**</u>

# His Stubborn Lover

# Excerpt

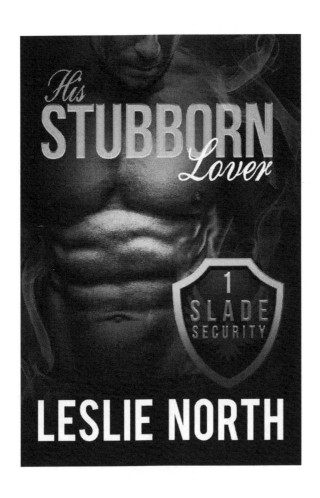

When your job is protecting people, the first rule is…never mix business with pleasure.

Keira Mantz has been given the job of a lifetime, and she refuses to fail. Trained as part of an elite security team, her first mission is to protect the Sheikh of Jawhara and his wife. What she thought would be a solo operation, though, is suddenly a two-person job. Her partner is none other than Brock Wells, the Viking-like team member who trained her. The last thing Keira wants is Brock stealing her thunder, but she'll do whatever it takes to succeed— even if it means pretending to be in love.

When Brock finds Keira in a bar fight and offers her a place on the team, he knows she is the right choice. With her mile-long legs, fierce determination, and unwavering focus, he has no doubt she can hold her own. But with the threat to the Sheikh closer than they realized, Brock has no choice but to intervene. To give them the cover they need, they'll have to act like they're a couple. Although Brock told himself he'd never get close to another woman, the job always comes first.

When their ruse becomes a little too real, can Keira and Brock risk letting their guards down, or will admitting their feelings put others' lives in danger?

Available now.

Brock Wells exited the bar, heading for his '66 Mustang. The twang of a sad love song followed him out, and his head buzzed with the four beers he'd had. The team had just finished a training operation in South America and Slade had given everyone some much needed time off—meaning Brock had come home hoping to find some female company.

He'd hit a bar that was a ways off from his usual haunts, looking for a stranger with doe eyes and a body that could make him forget just about everything. Tonight, however, his batting average was about as good as the one of whoever wrote that love song.

Well, it was probably better this way. Slade had no rules against team members getting hooked up outside of the teams, but he also didn't like sending anyone into the thick of things if they had attachments. That was where Brock liked to be—in the middle of the worst trouble. This meant that Brock liked his girls for one night only, and every girl in that bar had had the hungry look of a woman hunting a man.

It looked like it was going to be an early night with the UFC channel and a few more beers for him.

Glimpsing movement from the corner of his eye—three figures under the glare of the parking lot lights—Brock stopped, and everything else went into automatic assessment. Some habits never went away, and the ones from his days as a SEAL were deeply ingrained.

Two guys, one woman—and yeah, he wasn't being paid by Slade for this one, but he also wasn't wired to look away. He headed over, took up a spot that gave him the advantage, since it put him right behind the guy holding the knife, and boxed the trio against a battered pickup. He offered a friendly grin. "Looks like a party."

The two guys—good ol' boys by the looks of the wife-beater shirts and sagging jeans, and none too smart to go by the eyes glazed by drink and drugs—glanced at each other. The guy without a knife nodded at the half-empty parking lot. "Get lost."

Brock shrugged to loosen his shoulders. "Let the girl go and I won't have to mess up this crappy spot with your even crappier blood. I'm only asking once."

The girl had guts enough. She kept hold of one guy's wrist—the guy with the knife—but she glanced at Mr. Mouthy and said, her voice low and firm, "Please, I changed my mind, Toad."

"Toad?" Brock laughed. "Seriously, dude? That's your handle? Okay, we're done here." He brought his hand down on the shoulder of the guy with the knife—hard enough for the guy to let out a grunt.

Brock spun him around, punched him once in his soft gut. Not smart, dude, to let yourself go like that. The guy doubled over, spilling out whiskey-soaked breath. Brock snapped the knife from the guy's limp hand. It clattered to the asphalt. A jerk back and the guy lay flat on the ground, on his back. Brock kicked the knife away and glanced at Toad—Mr. Mouthy. "You want a go? Your choice."

Before Toad could even bunch a fist, the girl hauled off, caught him in the throat with the flat of her hand, and drove a knee into his groin. The guy doubled over, and

Brock gave a sympathetic wince. She kicked up at his jaw with a boot, and Toad crumpled like a wad of toilet paper.

Leaving the two guys on the ground, Brock grabbed the girl's wrist. "Come on. Let's go before these two even think about trying a round two, or call for their buddies to come kick our asses."

He pulled her with him, sizing her up as he went. She had long, straight hair, hitting below her shoulders; looked brown, maybe dark brown in this light. He couldn't judge the color of her eyes, but they were big, dominating a narrow face. Pretty, he'd guess. A little too skinny. A baggy shirt hung down over her hips, hiding anything she might have for breasts, too, but she had great legs—long and lean and encased in tight jeans. Plus boots made for kicking.

"You okay?" he asked.

She nodded and let go of his hand to go around and get into his convertible. He lifted an eyebrow at that—maybe this kind of gutsiness had gotten her in trouble to start with. She didn't seem to mind jumping into a stranger's car, but then he wouldn't want to hang around either to see how Toad liked being kicked in the nuts.

He started up his car and headed for the highway. "Where do you live?" He asked, leaning over so she could hear him over the wind, which was a soft roar in his ears and a pressure on his cheeks.

She shook her head, captured her flying hair with a hand, and slanted him a look. "No one's ever done that before. No one's ever helped me out."

Brock grinned. "It's kind of what I do." He pulled out a card and slipped it to her. It had his name on it and the words, Slade Security. She ran her fingers over the card, and Brock's throat tightened. She had great hands—long fingers, tapering, slim, and strong wrists. He liked the way she moved them, too, slow and certain. They reminded him, somehow, of white butterflies.

She looked at him again. "What kind of security?"

He shrugged. "Whatever anyone needs. Systems. Bodyguards. Surveillance. You name it. Slade, he's my boss, runs a full service operation."

She nodded, shifted so she faced him. "You military?"

"Used to be. Navy. I'm out now." She nodded again and grabbed her flying hair, yanking it back into a pony tail. He put his eyes on the road. He was not going to think about taking her back to his hotel room. Well, okay, he was going to think about it; but he was also going to remember her kicking a guy in the balls. "What about you?" he asked. "Figure out an address where you want me to take you?"

She shook her head. "My cousins set me up to work for Toad. They didn't tell me he wanted to have me selling drugs—and myself."

"Ah," Brock said, and gave a nod. "That accounts for the parking lot disagreement. No folks?"

"Not that I want to see." She faced the road, too. He could tell that from the way the car seat squeaked. "Don't have anything else going for me, either."

He glanced at her again. The light from the dash played over her face. She had brown eyes to match her hair; big eyes in a narrow, heart-shaped face. She'd also held up well in that parking lot, better than most would, and she'd known how to fight. That was a point in her favor. She also wasn't shaking or crying now. He liked that. "Where'd you learn to punch like that?" he asked.

She grinned. "Streets. Where else?"

"The streets. Meaning you fight dirty. That's cool. You want a job?" The words popped out, and Brock wanted to kick himself. That's what happened after four beers—impulse took over and his mouth went on auto-pilot.

He hadn't meant to get into this with her. He'd been taught to protect those around them. The weak. The misfortunate. The ones you loved. Those were the rare ones. He'd always had to watch out for the folks who needed someone. He'd always hated the idea of meeting his maker on foreign soil and having that tear someone up back home—and it had ended up costing him.

But Slade was looking to expand the teams with support staff. Slade had said he also wanted to get some females on board. There were some jobs that needed a woman to do things that a guy couldn't, like follow a female suspect or a client into a bathroom. Slade wasn't the kind of guy to put women in danger, but the truth was that females could be a great distraction. He glanced at the girl—yeah, he'd bet she'd clean up to be totally distracting.

She hadn't said anything, and he wasn't sure if that was because she hadn't heard him or was thinking things over. He was about ready to write her off—and that was a relief—when she asked, "What's the pay?"

He glanced at her. It was her call to dive into this, and Slade would make sure she stayed safe. She'd get training. She'd never go out without back up. That actually might be something this girl could use. If he left her on the streets, there'd be no telling what might become of her. He gave a nod. "Good. Really good."

She stuck out her hand. "I'm Keira Mantz. I don't use drugs and I don't sell them. I'm not up for anything illegal and I have no intention of ever being anyone's property!"

She had enough aggression in her tone that Brock shook his head. But he also grabbed her hand and shook it. She had a firm grip. "Well, don't go all Amazon man-hater on me."

"Why not?"

He glanced at her. Her mouth had twisted into a grimace, and he figured something had put her off men in general. Maybe Toad—or maybe just guys like him. Pity about that, but it'd be better for the job if she wasn't there to snag a guy. "Okay, go ahead with that. I can't guarantee anything, but I can take you to meet Slade. He's got to make the final call on you working for him. You want to stop and pick up anything before we head out to meet up with him?"

She shook her head. "I'm more than ready to leave my old life behind. All of it."

Brock put his eyes on the road. He knew about that. Sometimes life just got shitty enough that all you could do was leave the wreckage behind. He pulled out his cell phone to call Slade and set up a meet. The corner of his mouth twitched. Slade was going to love this girl—he just knew it. Brock snuck one more glance at her.

If she was coming on board with Slade's team, that put her off limits. Totally. Pity about that, because Brock wouldn't have minded seeing what she looked like under that big shirt of hers. But work came first. Always. That was one rule Brock was never breaking.

# His Stubborn Lover

# Excerpt

Available now.

Made in the USA
Middletown, DE
28 June 2018